PEARLHANGER

She swayed in with a tray holding a teapot, two cups, some gin and eight tonics. I showed her Donna Vernon's list of places.

'What are these places, love? Mini-Stone-henges? Druidical haunts? Ley lines?'

'They're simply places, Lovejoy.'

Just when I thought I'd cracked it. 'Nothing specially supernatural?'

'About Nottingham?' She smiled at that, lovely and fresh. 'My third husband came from Nottingham.' She looked at her tray, and down at me. 'What do you want first, Lovejoy? A drink, education about the supernatural or . . .?'

PEARLHANGER

A Lovejoy narrative

Jonathan Gash

ARROW

Arrow Books Limited
20 Vauxhall Bridge Road, London SW1V 2SA

An imprint of the Random Century Group

London Melbourne Sydney Auckland
Johannesburg and agencies throughout
the world

First published by William Collins Sons and Co. Ltd 1985
Hamlyn Paperbacks edition 1986
Arrow edition 1986
Mysterious Press edition 1987
Reprinted 1989 and 1991
7 9 11 12 10 8 6

Printed and bound in Great Britain by
Cox & Wyman Ltd, Reading, Berkshire

ISBN 0 09 941730 8

FOR

A story for Lal, Jackie, Yvonne, Elizabeth (who knows about this sort of thing), and Susan.

This book is dedicated, with respect and humility, to the Chinese God Wei D'to, who protects books from evil, destruction, and forgetful borrowers.

Lovejoy

CHAPTER 1

People are stupid: women with money, men with motorbikes, and everybody with pearls. To prove I'm in it too, this story starts in a seance.

It was a clear fraud (not me, the seance). The whole works, blackout, eight of us palms outspread and Owd Maggie in a shawl trying to disguise her Suffolk accent chattering to somebody called Cardew who wasn't there. I'm an antique dealer; this isn't my scene.

'Who's Cardew?' I asked Mrs Vernon, the woman I'd come with. Donna Vernon was blonde, intense, thirtyish, with a polyurethane prettiness, and had met me by arrangement that morning. I wasn't sure why. She had a faint transatlantic accent, almost completely concealed. I was intrigued. You don't get Yanks in East Anglia for the same reason we don't have Ethiopians.

'Shhh,' everybody went.

'Cardew Gaythorne,' Mrs Vernon whispered. 'Eighth-century squire from Lincoln.'

'Can't be,' I whispered back. 'The name's duff. Anyway, isn't he dead by now?'

'*Lovejoy*,' she ground out.

'Sorry, sorry.'

Why are women always so narked with me? Grumpily I shushed while the charade continued and the fat old bird prattled mystically on. I'd had enough of this, but Mrs Vernon was hanging on to every gasp. Also, she'd said she was hiring me. I wasn't banking on it because I'm used to failure. But missing the antiques auction down East Hill was getting me mad, bad news if you're penniless.

Antiques are all we have. They're all we can depend on

and the only things Mankind can look forward to. They deserve protection. I sighed the sigh of the antique dealer excluded from his rightful lust.

'You have a question, dear?' The seance führer had returned to earth with her normal harsh rasping voice.

Great. My chance. I brightened. 'Ta, Maggie. How come this Cardew bloke—?'

'*Lovejoy-I'll-not-tell-you-again,*' from Mrs Vernon. Me silenced, she put honey into her faintly American voice. 'Madame Blavatsky. We have a question for Cardew.'

Madame *Blavatsky*? That was a scream. Owd Maggie Hollohan used to keep the little health food shop by the war memorial selling skimmed milk and nuts, all those non-grub foods that make you hunger for the real thing. Nice old stick, but off her rocker. This seance business proved that. I've known her years. She was always fond of me, even gave me a pet nickname, Cockalorum.

'Please,' Mrs Vernon asked. 'Where is Sidney?'

'Cardew,' Owd Maggie intoned nasally. 'Where is Sidney?'

We waited a beat or two, some more breathlessly than others. I yawned.

'Well and happy,' Cardew said. I was disappointed. Cardew's voice was only Owd Maggie's voice pitched falsetto. Talk about phoney. She switched to her business voice again, presumably for speed. 'Sidney seeks great wealth.' I pricked up my ears. My boredom bottomed out and happiness seeped in. 'He will stay between the salt water and the sea sand.'

'How will I find him?' Mrs Vernon asked, quivering with eagerness.

'A man will be your guide,' Owd Maggie grated. She should have stuck to selling celery. As a medium she'd starve.

Undeterred, my trembling heroine drew breath for the biggie and demanded, 'Is Lovejoy the guide?'

'Here, nark it,' I said. 'Asking a ghost for a job's frigging ridiculous.'

'Shhh,' an elderly geezer croaked, fixing me through the gloaming with a specky stare. I don't really mind these phoney games, but being discussed with a phantom was bloody cheek. I let my attention wander.

Next to a dozing crone was a pleasant plumpish woman with that hint of succulence you always get in the overripe forties. Twice she'd looked away in the nick of time as I'd managed to raise my eyes from her lovely shape. The others were dried prunes, except for a bloke about thirty. Fair curly hair, weak face, casually dressed but uptight and looking very, very apprehensive. Funny how this rubbish gets to people. Maybe he was here to contact some ghost about an inheritance. Never once looked at me, though I had this odd feeling he was sussing me out in some way. I wish now I'd been more awake that morning.

'Cardew says it is him you do not trust.'

There was more of Owd Maggie's gunge. I won't go on about it if you don't mind. It's boring, and anyway I can't see what the point of a seance actually is. I mean to say, unless you're somebody with a supernatural bee in your bonnet like Mrs Vernon it's simply a weird fraud, right?

We escaped this let's-pretend just as the pubs opened. I didn't manage to get the plumpish bird's name and address. The surly old bloke with the specs and waistcoat was her hubby, a waste of space if ever I saw one.

Mrs Vernon led the way aggressively into a posh little café in our High Street. I was obviously in for a miserable confrontation over a tablecloth crushed by modern cutlery, my idea of purgatory. I knock everything over, and anyway posh nosh always leaves me hungry.

'Look, love,' I said as we entered. 'You've got it wrong. Spiritualism and me—'

'No, I haven't. You're to be my helper, Lovejoy. You heard Madame.' I'd explained it was only Owd Maggie shawled by candlelight but she wouldn't listen. Women are always dead certain about everything.

She did an odd thing as we went in. A tall man with close-cropped hair stepped out of the restaurant. He was nearly as scruffy as me, and wore a dishevelled anorak. I hadn't bumped into him or anything, yet Donna Vernon exclaimed, 'Mind, Lovejoy.' Curious. I'm clumsy, but not daft. 'Sorry,' I said to the bloke, whose eyes registered me, then Donna. 'Not at all,' he said in a BBC announcer's voice.

'There's another problem,' I confessed, sitting opposite her. The place was posh all right. Any minute and we'd be knee-deep in mulligatawny soup. 'I'm a bit short just now.'

'I'll pay, Lovejoy.'

'I've a few good deals on, though,' I lied briskly, feeling better.

She said calmly, 'You have one deal from now on. It's me. The rest are cancelled.' She smiled, quite a cold smile which announced my station in life: a serf. Here was a lady bent on getting her money's worth.

My face reddened. Women always put me down, just when I think I'm not doing so bad. Cancelling my costly deals was easy because I'd got none.

'What about your husband? I'm an antique dealer. Sounds as if you want the Old Bill.'

She passed me a menu, looking hard. 'Lovejoy, are you always shabby, or is today's outfit your tramp special?' Dead certain about everything and their voices carry. I reddened deeper as heads turned all across the restaurant.

'Ask Cardew,' I shot back.

She consulted a complicated gold wristwatch. 'I'm paying your salary from noon today, Lovejoy. You have one hour to finish sulking. Then we go.'

'To anywhere in particular?'

A waitress was poised for orders. With the innate perception of her kind she ignored me and focused on Mrs Vernon.

I said, 'Hello, Karen,' but she decided she wasn't acknowledging the town's riffraff today and gazed over my head.
Redderer and redderer. If it wasn't for women my life would
be tranquillity itself.

'We'll start with soup . . . ' my paragon began. I sighed.
Mulligatawny time. Quickly I ate both our rolls. I could
tell she was a born slimmer.

'I'll explain, Lovejoy. You are the only divvie in East
Anglia. I need your services.'

A divvie's a bloke who can recognize antiques by a kind
of clamorous sixth sense. It feels like a bell in my chest,
bonging at the genuine article. People often deny these
instincts exist—yet they believe in all kinds of daftness:
astrology, faith-healing, insurance, ghosts, omens, witches,
female intuition, politicians' promises—and fraudulent
Madame Blavatskys. Being a divvie's supposed to be a
miraculous stroke of good fortune, but so far it's only ever
brought me trouble—like good old Mulligatawny Vernon
here.

'My services? Let me guess.' If the restaurant was any
good they'd have brought some more rolls to keep us going
till the grub arrived. 'Your husband's replaced your family
heirloom with a replica. What was it? Painting? Bureau?'

'He has simply gone on a trip. I'm only interested in his
welfare, and I'll not have you maligning my family, Lovejoy.
Understand?'

Well, no, because a divvie's only good for antiques, not
people. But the soup came just then, saving me from sweeping out in a hungry huff. She gave me a list of places where
her husband had toured. Absently I stuffed it in my pocket.
The quicker we got this dreadful meal and the journey done
with, the quicker I could return to normality.

As I waded into my dainty grub praying it might at least
fill a dental cavity, I saw that fair-haired bloke from the
seance. He'd come into the restaurant and was ordering
from our upper-class hopeful Karen. He didn't even nod,

yet again there were strong vibes of awareness.

'Here, missus. D'you know him over there?'

She glanced with that studied slyness which women have perfected over the millennia: 'No, Lovejoy. Why?'

'He was at the seance.' I gave a chuckle. 'I'll pop back and ask Cardew about him, eh?' Donna Vernon said that wasn't funny. As it happens she was right, because I eventually did just that.

Like most smallish towns in East Anglia, we have no proper hotels, though every so often some tavern in the High Street gets a rush of blood to the head and announces that henceforth it will be called something like the Great Golden Pinnacle Hotel. Such ambition never lasts because everybody knows that it's really only the Hole In The Wall pub, and has been since before the Normans landed. Eventually the 'hotel' gives up pretending, lashes out on a tin of paint and sheepishly re-emerges as its old self. You can't change pubs any more than you can change people.

I tell you this small fact because it caused a pavement argument outside the Red Lion, and that set the seal on our mutual distrust, though I still say that the deaths weren't my fault.

'I have to check out of the hotel,' said my blonde.

To me that meant she was staying in Ipswich. 'Oh, right. See you tomorrow then, eh?'

'Where do you think you're going, Lovejoy?' She sounded and looked outraged. I'd started off down the pub yard. It's a short cut to Gimbert's auction rooms.

'Eh?'

She came at me blazing. 'Now you just look-a here, Lovejoy.' She honestly did say look-a. Her finger jabbed my chest. People stopped to listen and an infant in a pushchair applauded joyously. 'I want none of your male chauvinist fascism with me, do you hear?'

'Eh?' I thought: What the hell's she on about?

'I'm already packed, and you've got one hour—repeat, one—to be back right here. No play, no money. Understand?'

'Very well.' God, but she was annoying.

'And another thing.' She was pretty, but even thinking that was probably imperialism or something. 'Why did you steal that ashtray?'

I went all innocent. 'Ashtray?'

'In your pocket. You stole it right off that table.'

'You pretended you hadn't noticed,' I accused. It just shows how really sly women are deep down.

Since the National Bakelite collectors formed up, prices have gone through the ceiling. Luckily people have been slow to realize. Everybody thinks early plastics are simply breakable rubbish. Wrong. Jackson's restaurant has some ashtrays—ever fewer—which are Bandalasta, an early and valuable trade mark. Brittle, but costly. I could live half a week on the proceeds of my—well, Jackson's—ashtray.

'Personal reasons,' I said. I even bit my lip to show sincere remorse. It was my tenth stolen ashtray. I tried to look as though it was my first. 'Look, missus,' I said, going noble. 'My grandfather founded that restaurant. He built it with his own hands.' I showed her my own hands as proof. 'This is simply a souvenir. If you insist, I'll go back and pay for it. It's only plastic.' Neither of my grandads could boil an egg, let alone run a nosh bar.

'All right,' she said, slow but watchful. 'One hour exactly?'

'One hour,' I promised, and hurried off. Even if the entire frigging morning was wasted I was now free of that female nutter. Cheerfully I cut down past St Nicholas's churchyard and emerged into freedom near the Arcade. Alison Bannister beckoned from her antique shop—household furniture, mostly Victoriana, and dress items. I tapped my watchless wrist twice, promising to be with her by two o'clock, and hurried on. She had a militia man's antique 'housewife' I badly wanted—not a woman, but a tiny leather drawstring bag of threads, buttons, patches and sewing needles. I'd heard that Mankie Holland, he of the phoney catalogues and phonier eighteenth-century watercolours, had a buyer for one. Back to normality for that mighty antiques firm called Lovejoy Antiques Inc. The entire business is only me, but it's real honest-to-God living and that's more than you can say for any other form of existence. I trotted on to the auction, blissfully happy.

Seance indeed.

CHAPTER 2

Bliss. I inhaled the grotty armpit-and-dust stench of your typical country auction. Except some days everything goes wrong.

In the doorway somebody barged me. I swung angrily, saw who it was and grinned weakly. Big John Sheehan, with four homicidals. 'Wotcher, John,' I said. 'Sorry.'

'No harm done, Lovejoy,' he pronounced forgivingly. His serfs shoved me aside. I was relieved. John's a hard man, and I'm not. Tell you more about him later.

Worse, the flaming picture I wanted had gone—been sold, left me alone and palely loitering. Some rich undeserving swine had actually bid. I entered Gimbert's auction rooms furious with blondes, seances, auctions and auctioneers. I stormed through the crowd to where Margaret stood waiting for the good porcelain to come up. (In country auctions the best wine is always last; remember that tip and it'll save you money. The first couple of items are usually give-away cheapo, as come-ons.)

'Who got it, Margaret?'

Margaret Dainty turned calm blue eyes on me. 'First, good day to you, Lovejoy. Secondly, if you mean that Constable sketch, Gwen bought it. And she paid the earth. Where did you get to?'

'Seance. Where's Gwen gone?'

'Home to Bernard for her special reward.' Bernard and Gwen run a sex-encounter group, our current scandal. 'Did you say seance?'

I picked up the old dish Margaret had been inspecting and grumbled audibly, 'You should have bought that oil sketch instead of tarting around this gunge.' Saying those words broke my heart and mentally I whispered an apology to the dish, but casually I replaced it on its job-lot pile. Lot 228.

'Silence during the bidding, Lovejoy,' Wheatstone warbled from the rostrum. He's an import from Stortford, all chained spectacles and degrees in Fine Art, but at least he can read and write which for an auctioneer is space-age stuff. He resembles all auctioneers the world over: pin-stripe suit, slicked hair, and looks deep fried.

'Shut your teeth, Stonie.' I didn't even glance. Amid laughter and catcalls I nudged Margaret. We edged from the mob compressed round the podium. Jeb Spencer—antique jewellery, Regency fashions—and others were keeping an eye on me to see if my irritation about the Constable oil sketch was genuine.

'Silly bitch, Margaret. I told you to bid for it if I was delayed.' I spoke loudly for Jeb's benefit. His barker—Doris, a rheumy old doxy with radar ears—was shuffling innocently nearby.

Margaret looked harassed, not sure if I was pretending. 'You never said definitely, Lovejoy.'

I kept up the gripe. 'Bloody hell. Do I have to decide every single time there's a Constable copy around East Anglia? We're knee-deep in the sodding things . . .'

Doris trundled innocently back into the throng to report that I'd used that doom-word 'copy'. I breathed again. We were now in the space near the tea bar at the back. Margaret was curious, wondering what was going on. She's early middle age, lovely, has a gammy leg from some marital

campaign or other, and loves me. We've been intermittently
close for years because of our unspoken agreement: I never
ask after her husband, and she doesn't demand honesty
from me. This is why older women are best by miles. I'd
swap ten popsies for one thirty-plus any day of the week.

'Get somebody to bid for 228,' I muttered, still pretending
anger for Jeb Spencer's benefit.

'Who?' Margaret knew better than to glance back to
where 228 lay. Idly I scanned the mob of dealers. God, but
we look horrible in a group. Tinker was there, an old bloke
milling about a cluster of overcoated dealers. He's my own
barker, paid in solid blood to sniff out antiques, rumours of
deals, any news at all, and sprint—well, totter—to me with
the news. He's a filthy old soldier. His cough can waken the
dead.

'Flag Tinker down. Tell him to get one of his old mates
in from the betting shop, sharpish. His mate can have the
rest of the job lot, but keep the Arita dish.'

'Isn't it a bit Chinese for Arita?'

The big dish had the Dutch East India Company 'VOC'
mark among its stylized pomegranate designs—the O and
C each bestriding one limb of the V in a central circle—all
in underglaze blue. The Dutch wanted replacements for the
Chinese porcelains they couldn't get after 1658, and began
their Japanese Arita shipments about then. A genuine one
like 228 can keep you two months in sinful luxury.

'You women always bloody argue. Dutch VOC Arita's
supposed to be Chinese Wan Li style. Japanese potters spent
half a century perfecting the phoney look.'

'Did it feel genuine, Lovejoy?'

'Yes.'

'All right.' And from the way she spoke I knew she'd now
arrange a serious bid. She trusts my divvying skill implicitly,
though not much else. 'Is Gwen's Constable sketch genuine?'

'Genuine old, not genuine Constable.'

Margaret pulled a face. 'People were saying it was a Tom Keating fake.'

'I know.' I knew because I'd started the rumour to lower the price. Tom was one of East Anglia's great modern success stories in fakery.

'Bernard will be pleased,' Margaret pronounced sweetly. Gwen's husband gambles every groat Gwen brings home. It's quite an arrangement. Actually I like Gwen, but she gets on Margaret's nerves. 'Seances, Lovejoy? Not Beatrice, I trust.' Beatrice is our one antiquarian occultist and lives down on the wharf with a giant mariner. She and I used to, erm, before the Navy arrived.

'No. Owd Maggie. Some bird wanting news of an overdue husband.' I kept half an ear on Wheatstone's meanderings. 'A ghost told her to hire me.'

Margaret was interested. 'Is he dead?'

'The ghost presumably; the husband hardly. Owd Maggie said he was living it up at the seaside.'

'And you won't go?'

I shrugged. 'Got fed up. No point. He's probably just shacked up with some tart, keeping his head down and his—'

'Lovejoy,' Margaret reproved, taking my arm all the same. I shook free and gave her the bent eye. In antiques there's no time to be pally.

'They're at lot 203. Get a move on.'

She tutted in annoyance and moved over to the mob for Tinker. The old bloke was the right choice. Nothing daunts porcelain experts more than finding a scruff bidding confidently alongside. For a few pints Tinker'd bid serenely for the Mona Lisa. Probably had, in fact, more than once.

Pleased at having rescued the day from total waste, I ambled, grinning, to get a cup of tea and be ready for the fun. The other dealers were all suspicious. Helen lit a cigarette and eyed me sardonically, knowing something was up but having to guess exactly what. She's the shapeliest legs in the business and coughs in her sleep from so many fags. Patrick, our most extravagant local, was also suspicious. He looks and is decidedly eccentric, but he and Lily—a wealthy married lady he archly describes as his procuress—are a pair of formidably shrewd dealers. Big Frank from Suffolk, terror of local silver collectors and marriageable spinsters, feverishly rummaged through his catalogue in case he'd missed something. He's our most-married dealer, seven on the trot plus one foreign bigamy on a Beirut package tour, though we'd all warned him not to go.

Cheerfully I sank back on a Windsor wheelback chair— modern copy, real gunge, not even a proper yew-wood hoop to grace its poor little back—and felt my spirits rising. What with a chipped cup of grotty peat-coloured tea, a warehouseful of antiques and junk, amid a mob of idiot dealers and the scatterbrained old public, I felt able to reflect on the perfection of life.

'Here, Lovejoy. I've an old print covered in candlegrease.' Rudyard Mannering had sidled up from the intense mob of dealers. He's a bloke who always looks suspicious even if he's doing nothing wrong, although I like him. He's quite harmless. All he thinks of is old manuscripts. He hovered furtively, a Bolshevik bomb-carrier if ever I saw one.

'Scrape it with a paper-knife, then soak it in petrol a few minutes. Use BP Five Star. Have you a camel-hair brush . . . ?'

Absolute bliss.

My ecstasy ended exactly at Lot 217, a Victorian chaise-longue with faded upholstery and one leg missing, because Donna Vernon found me, like a whirlwind. See what I mean about women being really selfish? Just because her husband's gone missing she comes and interrupts my day.

From then on it was downhill to doom all the way, and no turning back. God knows I tried.

★

Her abuse and threats came about half-and-half. Of course everybody had a laugh at my expense, especially when Wheatstone had his whizzers—auctioneer's assistants, even more cretinous—bundle me and the blonde into the glass-partitioned office. My mates kept grinning through the glass pulling flat-nosed faces. Chris Bonnington, he's coins and Tudor domestic crafts, even opened the door to call some good-humoured jest but by then I'd had enough and gave him one of my looks. He left in silence.

No silence about Donna. She threatened me with sub-poenas, writs, lawsuits, hate, poverty, and took a swing at me. I countered by shoving her into Wheatstone's one chair.

She yelped, squirming. 'That's assault and battery! Chauvinist pig! I'll sue you—'

'Law's irrelevant to such as me, love.' I kept her pinned down with Lot 331, silver-headed walking cane, quite nice but a bit late with its Birmingham hallmark of 1883. Her belly was too soft to damage the tip so that was all right. 'Just get somebody else.'

'I'll see you never work again, Lovejoy!'

'Thanks.' I've not done an honest day's work for years. Somebody on my side at last.

The door opened, and in wafted Lydia on a cloud of babble from the auction, her face screwed up to denote how sternly she was taking this spectacle.

'What's going on, Lovejoy?' She's only my apprentice, but you wouldn't think it from the way she goes on some-times. She's a born nuisance, but great. Heart of a sinner, soul of a nun. Martin Luther knew his stuff. This voluptuous maid wears morality like an erotic gymslip.

'You're a witness!' cried my blonde. 'Lovejoy attacked me.'

I transformed instantly. 'Mrs Vernon wants me to go away with her, Lydia,' I said meekly. 'I don't want to go.'

'Pull yourself together, madam,' Lydia commanded, cold. 'I will not have hysteria.'

Mrs Vernon stopped wriggling at the wintry tone. I'd chosen my phrases carefully. Ben, one of Gimbert's whizzers, rapped on the glass for the cane. Gingerly I relaxed pressure and passed Lot 331 out of the door, spotting the relief on Big Frank's face. Women always like hearing that a man can't stand another bird, even if it's only one of those telly newsreaders with disastrous hairdos.

'Lovejoy's under contract to me and's trying to default.' Mrs Vernon rose to do battle. I was happy to see she was now furious at Lydia instead of me. I edged out of the door. Women, especially real ones like Lydia, have this knack of quelling opposition by simple turns of phrase. It's a gift. God really knew His stuff with spare ribs.

Jeb Spencer and Chris were closer to the glass partition than they needed to be, and moved aside with studied casualness. The sods had been trying to listen.

'A rich London buyer,' I lied casually.

They tried to nod disbelief but I could see they were unsure. Pleased, I saw Margaret leave carrying a bag. Tinker must have nobbled the job lot with the Arita dish. That meant ten per cent, say, a week's living expenses from the VOC plate alone after the split. I'd see Margaret got her favourite reward. Now to con the near-Constable oil sketch out of Gwen Pritchard before husband Bernard pleasured it off her and gambled it on some lame nag, and I'd be laughing.

There was a commotion by the door. Algernon was arriving in his Martian-style bike rig. Algernon's my other apprentice, buck teeth, clumsy and mindbendingly slow, for whom I'm paid a pittance to teach antiques. He has the brains of a rocking-horse. He was looking pleased with himself as he blundered through the door and fell over a small escritoire with a crash. The dealers laughed. He's never done anything right yet, so why change the habit of a lifetime?

'Lovejoy!' he yelped, grinning delightedly as an old dear hauled him to his feet. 'That pewter!'

Disbelievingly I thought: I'll cripple him. It was supposed to be a secret deal, the nerk. Subtle as the Blitz. This was obviously turning out to be one of those days. I darted through the mob at a breathless run into the safety of Gimbert's yard.

Fourteen pubs within a stone's throw. One gulp of the town's exhilarating smog and I headed towards the Three Cups and perdition.

Ten minutes later I was pulling Owd Maggie's leg about being a witch. She drinks foul black stout until the pub closes.

'Madame Blavatsky, I presume,' I joshed. 'What'll Cardew have? Pint?'

She spoke without animosity, contentedly hunched in the inglenook. 'You can scoff, Cockalorum. But he's as real as you or me.'

I pretended to be impressed. 'Is Cardew always right?'

'Never wrong, dear.' She rattled her glass. I scraped together the odd groat and fetched her a bottle. 'He was right about you,' she pointed out. 'Told that lady straight, Cardew did. Said you were not to be trusted.'

'Then Cardew's a cheeky sod. Anyhow, he got it wrong. I'm not going.'

'Lovejoy.' Breathlessly Lydia slid into the seat beside me as I spoke.

'Got rid of her, eh?' I was really pleased, though surprised Lydia had entered the tavern alone. She usually knocks at the door and waits to be brought in, going red and keeping her eyes on the floor. This time she was ignoring our tawdry surroundings. If anything, she was a bit pale around the gills. My heart sank.

'You've sold me to white slavers,' I accused.

'No, Lovejoy. Please listen. Good afternoon, Madame Blavatsky.'

'Hello, love,' said Owd Maggie, smiling at me. I could

have throttled her, batty old knowall.

'There's been a prediction. In a dream. Mrs Vernon received a warning. You must go with her, Lovejoy.'

I tried to push off but Lydia was penning me in. Luscious women are a right pest. 'For crying out loud. This isn't the frigging Dark Ages, Lydia. Everybody knows superstition's all crap.'

'Kindly moderate your language, Lovejoy,' Lydia said. 'No situation's too horrible for good manners.'

'You tell him, dear,' from Maggie. 'He can't go against the guidance.'

'Shut your gums, you silly old crab. You've caused enough trouble.'

'Lovejoy! Apologize this instant!'

I mumbled something to mollify Lydia but I could tell her heart wasn't in all this.

'You *see*, Lovejoy. You are our only dealer who has the inner eye.'

'I divvie antiques, not people.'

'Cardew knows,' from Owd Maggie.

I wondered for a second if Cardew secretly told her what me and Lydia got up to, blow-by-blow accounts as it were.

'But Mrs Vernon hates me. And she's going to sue.'

'Not now I've negotiated a lucrative rate.'

See what I mean about women? Sniffing heartbreak because I was in chancery, meanwhile briskly fixing percentages.

'Don't be cross, Lovejoy,' she urged earnestly. 'I have ensured that you will reside only in first-class accommodation, receive intermittent emoluments, and any antique purchases—'

'Antiques?' I perked up in spite of Lydia's Brontëspeak. Until now there'd only been talk of this tiresome husband.

Lydia's eyes opened wide. 'Didn't you know? Mrs Vernon's husband is an antique dealer on an antiques sweep through East Anglia. The idea is you simply find him—'

'—through the antique shops he visited?' I yelped. My spirits soared. I assumed a quiet courage. 'Very well, er, darling. If . . . if it will please you.'

'You're so sweet,' she said. Because it was true I let her buy the next round. The search couldn't take long, after all. And if we already had a list of places where he'd gone, it'd be simple.

Right?

CHAPTER 3

Next morning dawned wet and gale force across the estuary. A strong turbulence was whistling up the valley tumbling my apples on to the grass. Lydia had arrived early, shivering and complaining whenever the wind gave its chimney moan. Her feet are always perishing cold, worse than Dolly's and Connie's even in summer. She's unreal, a gentle little soul full of vitamins, Victorian manners and bran flakes, and was packing for Armageddon.

'Your brown pullover if it's chilly, Lovejoy,' she was saying, folding away. 'Shirts and underpants. Shaver, Lovejoy. Look.'

To oblige I looked. Face screwed in solemn concentration, she deposited my electric razor with the deliberation of a stage magician trying to convince a sceptical audience he's not cheating. 'Right,' I said.

Lincoln. Lowestoft. Manningtree. Surely not in that order? I had drawn rings round the places on the map from the list Donna Vernon had given me in Jackson's restaurant. East Anglia's a big place; admittedly no Australia, but more nooks. Purling Lock. Where the hell was Purling Lock? Barnthwaite I'd never heard of and couldn't find.

Surprisingly, Donna Vernon appeared almost at ease and really rather presentable when finally she showed. I hadn't looked too hard at her yesterday. I vaguely remembered an assortment of modern stridey gear, the jeans and duffel sort, all buckles. Her hair now moved a bit instead of seeming clamped. Her coat was actually brightly coloured. Today's mouth was an obvious red, whereas yesterday I'd only noticed the decibels.

'Good morning, Lovejoy,' she said to me out of the car window. Lydia got a curt nod.

'A couple of last-minute's, Lydia.' I humped my case in. 'Tell Helen her price is too high for that Ming dynasty erotic print of that couple on the matting. Get Patrick to go halves with us for Gwen's *Landscape Noon* sketch that she got yesterday, and fend Jessica off over that Nabeshima porcelain. She can have our Lowestoft jug, but charge her the earth.'

'Very well.' Lydia stood there on the gravel outside my cottage door. 'You have everything.' Unquestioning statement, that. 'Travel safely . . .'

'Not be long.'

'Let's get this show on the road, for God's sake!' from dearest Donna.

As we slithered out into the lane scattering pebbles I saw Lydia's hand raised in the minutest flutter. It takes somebody as sensitive as me to realize what an effort that gross demonstration cost her. I cleared my throat. Women get to you. You have to take proper precautions because female means sly. I'd have to watch myself. Antiques is too grim a game for attachments.

Algernon had just got off the village bus by the chapel. He saw me and flagged us down, spooking a fat pony which was noshing the chapel hedge. He goggled in the car window.

'Lovejoy! There you are! How very fortunate—'

'Cut it. You got the pewter medallions?'

Mrs Vernon drummed her fingers on the steering-wheel. He was astonished. 'Lydia didn't inform you?'

'Of what?' Foul suspicions welled within my breast—see how catching fancy talk is?

He stepped back, smirking proudly. 'I did what you continually instruct, Lovejoy. I *checked*! The Latin inscriptions were gibberish!'

'And you didn't fetch them,' I registered brokenly.

'True!' Algernon exclaimed in triumph.

'Drive on, missus.' I wound the window shut.

The motor moved out on to the main road, leaving the nerk babbling inanities in the exhaust fumes.

'You're a chauvinist bastard, Lovejoy.'

'What *is* that?' I was honestly interested.

'Shakespeare's daughter wasn't even taught to write. *That*'s chauvinism!'

'You mean she never learned.' I thought: Clever old Judith Shakespeare. Sounded to me as if Big Bill's offspring had her head screwed on. Everybody'd expect her to produce *Hamlet Rides Again* the first rainy weekend. I went on the attack to suss Donna out. 'Where do you Yanks stable your horses if you've got no old cathedrals, love?'

She checked the rear-view mirror. 'That young man saved you a fortune, and you treat him like dirt.'

I stared. People just can't be this dim. 'Those medallions were Billie and Charlie fakes, eighteenth-century, rare, and pricey. A lunatic caftan-wearing lentil-eating clock collector called Mannie down at Wivenhoe had three of them and had agreed to let me have them on split commission. Now Algernon's ballsed it up.'

Mrs Vernon's glance raked me briefly. 'I get it, Lovejoy. Everybody else is always wrong, except you. That it? You're great, the rest morons?'

'You're brighter than I thought.' I was surprised. She was coming on.

'What are you about, Lovejoy?'

Time for the yap-and-guess interlude, evidently. 'Me? Antiques.'

'A person can't only be about antiques.'

I gave her one of my force eight glances so she'd know I meant it. 'If I'd claimed to love money, rape or Olympic yachting you'd believe me. Or,' I added drily, 'ghosts.'

She was too angry to contradict my misuse of the term. 'You're a put-down pig,' she said, her face pale with fury.

'Drop me at the next corner, please.'

Interestedly I watched the fascinating inward struggle. Women are always like this to some degree, aching to belt you one yet simultaneously wanting to use you in their designs. I'd been clocked by better women than her, so that was nowt new. The real question was, what was her particular design? The plot thickened around us as she pulled in to the pavement opposite a toffee-shop and cut the engine. Her breathing showed no sign of returning to normal. She finally started without it.

'Lovejoy. You're an anti-feminist pig. But I'm stuck with you.'

'Not necessarily.' I was all reason.

She commanded, 'You listen. I've a husband to find. You're hired to—'

'Shhh, Donna.' I talked on into her astonished rage. 'Difficult for a woman to be a frigging bore, but you made it. Just look at you. Your coat's imitation Shetland. Your buttons are imitation bone. Your cotton's faked cotton. Your cardigan's imitation lambswool. Your shoes are imitation leather. Ditto for your handbag, purse, that Aran of yesterday, knickers too I shouldn't wonder. Your plastic bloody bangle's even fake plastic.' And would you believe she still didn't throw me out? Her endurance fascinated me more and more. 'The real question is what Donna Vernon's about, isn't it?'

Her lips were a pale mauve set among white lines. One of those Venetian carnival masks, grotesque stasis but with a lot going on behind if you risk a look in the eyes. Her silent lips moved, presumably a command to explain. I'd made a right friend here. Yet again. 'I can't quite decide, Donna,' I concluded with a winning smile. 'You're a scream. All that spiritualism gunge to convince me you were so unsure about hiring me. You'd decided on me long before you crossed Owd Maggie's mit with silver. And.'

'And?' Furiously whispered, just audible.

'And what's the game, Donna? TTS? Treasure Tax Shelter?' She looked puzzled. 'A row with hubby hoovering up the antiques for himself? He nicked your favourite sports car? Taken the next-door blonde as footwarmer? Which is it?'

The Treasure Tax Shelter began in her own back yard. It's usually based on investors clubbing together to finance Caribbean galleon-hunters, but any old priceless treasure will do—as long as your own particular Inland Revenue Service agree on that elusive definition of 'treasure'. It's finders keepers. If your spade turns up nothing all year, your investment is written off as expenses. If you find a *Mary Rose* or *Santa Margarita*, then you decide what percentage of the bullion will be called 'profit', and gracefully allow that slender margin to be taxed. (Get it? The rest of the bullion you keep as 'expenses', heh-heh.) But what exactly *is* treasure? An Old Master painting in a pawnshop? A Hester Bateman silver table-centre on open view at a London auction? A pair of tulip-wood wings for a 1911 French monoplane? Answer: yes to all. Since that magic day in 1980 in Key West where modern TTS came down from heaven, it's been heap big monetary medicine.

And Donna didn't know what it was. Now, even our home-grown antique dealers, legendary scoopers of the Nobel for collective idiocy, have heard of it.

Therefore she was no antique dealer.

And collectors are merely antique dealers plus a limited amount of cerebral cortex. Therefore she was no collector.

Therefore it was the next-door-blonde syndrome or the please-return-the-Jaguar-darling bit. Yet was Donna the

sort to leave her car keys on any bloke's keyring? Hardly.
For my money she was the sort to help an erring hubby on
his way by firing him and his blonde from a cannon.

Therefore . . .?

I realized I'd run out of therefores when she lowered her
eyes and lied, 'You're right, Lovejoy. That's it. A treasure
tax shelter scheme.'

With difficulty I didn't thrombose at her fib. I'd have to
sort it out later. In the dark hours sometimes I wish I wasn't
so thick.

'All right.' I went all cherubic. 'Now I know, I'll help you
to trail your lord and master.'

'You arrogant sexist chauvinist pig.'

This sort of reaction puzzles me. People always want me to
behave like a video game. 'Isn't everybody?' I was honestly
asking her but she didn't speak again until we were bowling
down the A12 bypass.

'Will that possessive bitch back there in your shit-awful
cottage fix all those deals?'

That narked me still further. 'And twelve others. By
weekend.' She would, too.

My employer was smiling unpleasantly. 'Let's hope she
gets the right sketch, Lovejoy. The unique one sold at
Gimbert's yesterday was a sketch of *The Haywain,* Constable's most famous painting with the wagon crossing the
pool. You even said its name wrong.'

It's one of life's greatest tragedies that antique dealing,
handling and caring for the loveliest creations of Man, lies
in the hands of cretinoids who can't tell the difference
between a Brabant rose-cut diamond and a light bulb.
There's not a neurone among the lot.

'You're brainy, missus. Too brainy to know that John
Constable called his painting *Landscape Noon.* The wagon
you mentioned is properly called a scarf. And it isn't crossing
the pool. Look at the painting. You'll see there's no road.
The wagoneer's driven into the pool to soak the wheels. And

the oil sketch isn't unique. Constable himself did at least
five. Round these parts rumour says his son John also did
maybe seven more. Shall I go on?' I settled down. 'Wake
me when you stop for coffee, missus.' I gave a theatrical
snore. This relationship was going downhill. Driving ten
minutes and already on our third row. Even marriages last
longer.

'You just boobed, Lovejoy.' She was smiling-not-smiling,
teeth bared at the windscreen. 'You just threw your day's
pay out the window.'

'Like this?' I reached across, waggled the steering-wheel
to free the ignition key, and lobbed the key out. The motor
whined with horrible shrillness. We careered obliquely
across the carriageway. Donna struggled to correct us,
screaming. I cowered in my seat as we slammed the crash
barrier.

Horns blared. I'd no idea there were so many sorts. No
wonder they're a big collecting item. We bumped against
the grass verge, rocked to stillness. Silence.

I was out in a flash, darting among the traffic. The Old
Bill would come wah-wahing along any minute. I climbed
the crash barrier and began to walk briskly back towards
town. Other cars had stopped, the motorists standing out
looking, nosey sods.

It was typical of Donna Vernon's whole daft escapade
that the one vehicle to stop wasn't some kindly wagon driver.

'Coo-ee, cherub!' My heart froze. 'Lovejoy!'

I thought: Oh God, no, please. Not now. Not me. But
there the grotesque giant car stood in all its glitterglare glory
with Sandy waving from its window. In a panic I scanned
the road searching for somewhere to hide, forests, a barn,
anywhere. Nothing. Miserably I walked off the verge cursing
my luck.

'Times hard, Lovejoy?' Sandy trilled. 'I know *exactly* how
you *feel*! I've spent positive *æons* trolling this bypass, dear!'

'Wotcher, lads. Erm . . .' The enormous Rover was a

right spectacle. Not a garish colour missing. Silver leaves
twined round scarlet zigzags, green sunbursts, glittering
fluorescent blues and yellows. Even the tyres were sparkling,
gold dots on purple. A long tasselled fringe fibrillated its
primrose lurex round the roof. Sequins shimmered over the
bonnet.

Mel was sitting in the passenger seat, arms folded. My
heart sank further. They'd had another row. An approaching
car slowed, Donna Vernon at the wheel. Quickly I opened
the Rover's door and got in. 'Ta, Sandy.' I peered nervously
over my shoulder as I sank into the interior's magenta
leather.

'Oooh!' Sandy squealed delightedly. 'Lovejoy's escaping
again!' He turned into the oncoming traffic, serenely
acknowledging the furious cacophony by a regal wave of his
mink-gloved hand. He was wearing a sequined smock and
a magnolia bertha. 'Don't blame you, dearie,' Sandy said.
'She looked a right mare. Has naughty Lovejoy been dipping
his little wick where he oughtn't?'

I went red. You can see why they embarrass even an
impoverished hitch-hiker. 'Nothing like that,' I said. 'She
wants me to do a job, that's all.'

'You mean you're *not* for hire, Lovejoy?' He was tittering.
'A record!' I swear he loves trouble.

'Look. Can you give me a lift to Beatrice's?'

'No,' Mel said sullenly, fuming about something. 'I hate
her. Phoney.'

'Of course we will, cherub.' Sandy giggled, darted a
malevolent glance at his partner. 'Having your little pinkie
read, dear? Beatrice is frightfully good. She did me—and I
do mean my horoscope. Promised ever so many naughty
things.' He gave a roguish wink over his shoulder and said
innocently, 'Didn't she, Mel? Said I was going to meet a
tall dark stranger. He's not turned up yet, but I live in
hope.'

'Will you stop chattering?' from Mel.

Sandy trilled, 'Mel's in a *mood*, Lovejoy. He ordered yellow ochre curtains for our dear little motor. Can you imagine? I *had* to change them. Don't you agree?'

'Er,' I said, looking at the frills that adorned each car window. 'Well, er, I've never seen plum-striped orange lace before . . .'

That started them bickering all the way down the river estuary.

'We've been to a wedding, Lovejoy,' Sandy cooed, darting Mel a malicious look. 'One of Mel's old friends.'

'You were hateful,' stonily from Mel.

'It was *divine*, Lovejoy! The bride (her friends kept calling her that) wore a bullet-proof Laura Ashley long tight sleeves I mean lace—*lace*!—on seersucker how original to be so *wrong* and white too . . .' Tittering, he maintained the flow of spite while Mel fumed.

I'm never sure about this weird pair. Mel is glass, porcelain and art up to Art Deco. Sandy prefers eastern antiques and household wares up to Ted the Seventh, though Sandy always says he can be bought off with candy. They live in our village, with an open-floored barn for antiques behind their house. Their whole parade is silly, yet they drive the hardest antique bargains in East Anglia. Sandy says they're two sheep in wolf's clothing.

Ten-thirty and they dropped me at the wharfside cottage where Beatrice lives. I was on tenterhooks.

'You can pay for the lift,' Sandy said as I stepped out among the lobster pots and nets. 'Divvie a Palissy for Mel. Promise?'

'It's genuine,' Mel said, sulking.

'Right,' I agreed, wavering hungrily. A Palissy is a coloured lead-glazed earthenware piece, rare and valuable but gruesome as only a sixteenth-century Frenchman can make it. Each piece that Bernard Palissy made is decorated with snakes, lizards, dead fish and God-knows-what. Naturally, art turned swiftly to roguery, and cackhanded copies were made for at least three centuries. We'd had a number of the worst—Portuguese—turn up lately. I felt sure Mel had got one of these gungey items in a job lot. The Mafra family in Caldas rattled them off till 1887.

A few wharfsiders and fishermen were goggling at the monstrous motor and its exotic occupants in disbelief as I disembarked.

'Ta, lads,' I said. 'Let's hope Beatrice is in.'

'Always *is*, cherub,' Sandy trilled loudly. 'The question's in what.'

Mel joined in the fray with relish. 'And *do* say her red porch light's gone out, Lovejoy. She'll lose business.'

I heard Sandy's falsetto giggle all the way over the cobbles. My mind was reeling from the car's colours and their ridiculous talk. But my luck had changed. Beatrice was in, up, sober, conscious, alone, and momentarily celibate. An all-time first.

Wrong again, Cardew, I told him mentally as the door buzzed and I climbed Beatrice's stairs. I'd not gone with Donna Vernon, and I wasn't going either. If anything, I'd go after her hubby and his antiques on my own.

CHAPTER 4

An hour later Beatrice and I were shakily brewing up. Beatrice's antique shop is on the wharf of our tiny port, and mostly does ancient dolls and toys, now big money. Lately, her quarterly list had included items dealing with fortune-telling, tarot cards, ouija boards and whatnot. She calls herself an occultist. Other people, especially Mel and Sandy, don't. Beatrice always wears a ton of thick make-up plastered all over her face, really lovely. The kitchen's so full of those funny bottles women like that we had a hard time finding the tea-bags. She was slightly tipsy by then, and swayed more than ever at the ghastly notion of a non-alcoholic drink. The tea caddy had a layer of dust.

Yet Beatrice isn't the slattern I suppose I'm making her sound. She's honest and friendly, which goes a long way in my book. She fell for a coastal pilot and simply moved to where she would be the first thing he stepped on when coming ashore. We call him Barney because he's called Bill (get it? Barnacle Bill). Unkind friends claim she has telescopes at every window, but I say leave her alone. If loving was the worst thing we all did, the world wouldn't be such a bloody shambles.

In the post-loving doze my mind went awry. All that spooky lunacy at the seance, I suppose. It brought back that odd verse in Owd Maggie's gravelly voice. Stupid, because the only thing you find of any value between the salt water and the sea sand is pearls, not missing husbands. They say dreaming is dangerously close to madness. My slumbering brain jumbled signs of the zodiac, magical emblems and crystal balls, all into a great swirl, finally settling them into a distorted pattern with one giant pearl hanging there. Bea frightened me into palpitating wakefulness by tottering out, pulling on a silk dressing-gown full of zodiacal signs. A clue. Four of her rings, modern gunge alas, were also emblematic of unfathomable mystery.

'Here, Bea,' I called. I'd shot back to bed because her patch was warmer than mine. As well, from there you can see the small boats moving in the harbour. I wanted no sudden nauticals swaggering unexpectedly round the old bollards while I was engaged in psychic exploration. 'You in thick with Owd Maggie?'

'Madame Blavatsky? We're eight-in-the-ring sometimes. Why?'

Eight what? 'All true, is it?'

'Certainly. But some are more honest than others, some more gifted. You want milk in this brew, Lovejoy?' She gave a tiny distressful groan as the kettle whistled.

'Zodiacs, spiritualism, ghost-hunting, that Cardew gig. Is it all the same?'

'Certainly not.'

'Then come and educate me.'

She swayed in with a tray holding a teapot, two cups, some gin and eight tonics. I showed her Donna Vernon's list of places.

'What are these places, love? Mini-Stonehenges? Druidical haunts? Ley lines?'

'They're simply places, Lovejoy.'

Just when I thought I'd cracked it. 'Nothing specially supernatural?'

'About Nottingham?' She smiled at that, lovely and fresh. 'My third husband came from Nottingham.' She looked at her tray, and down at me. 'What do you want first, Lovejoy? A drink, education about the supernatural, or . . .?'

Spiritualism is different from astrology, I learned to my surprise. Futurism and ghost-hunting have little in common. And not only that. Beatrice went on to explain that a seance was a very special entity. It has definite purposes, set rituals. You just can't get a table, pull the blinds and start. Only ignoramuses assumed that all these were vaguely one and the same thing. She told me it all so matter-of-factly, as if it was jampacked full of self-evident truths, that I became quite narked and told her to knock it off.

'People often react like you, Lovejoy,' she told me. 'You don't *want* it to be true. And you're scared.'

'Scared? Me?' That really got me rolling in the aisles. I laughed loud and long.

'You, Lovejoy.' She poured a tumbler of gin and supported my head so we could both watch the harbour for Barnacle Bill's bobbing barque. 'It's perfectly natural to be apprehensive.'

'Look, Bea. The only thing I'm scared of is Barney

catching me here, and a deranged female called Mrs Vernon catching me anywhere.'

'Oh, Donna Vernon'll find you all right.'

'Like hell.' I'd said the words, smiling out at the grey sea and the Martello tower, before the penny dropped. 'Here. How did you know her first name?'

'Met her. Night before last. She came here asking where she could get a divvie.'

I shoved her away to sit up and look more directly. This was news. 'And you told her me?'

'Of course. I saw your face in conjunction with Mrs Vernon's. Simple. I gave her your address.'

'So she took me to Owd Maggie's to check.' Out there a small boat was passing the bar. It looked familiar. Nervously I said, 'That your bloke's boat, Bea?'

'Oh yes. He's early.' She toasted the distant craft delightedly with a tilt of her glass.

Ever since these bloody women had started on this fortune-telling lark I'd been in a continual state of alarm. I scrabbled for my clothes effing and blinding. 'Couldn't you have warned me, you silly cow?'

'The unexpected's always at hand, Lovejoy. It's in ourselves we must look.'

'Tell Barnacle Bill that,' I said fervently. He'd done over a Wivenhoe bloke once for snogging with Bea in her car. It hadn't been a pretty sight.

'Don't you want to know your prediction, Lovejoy?' she asked in all innocence while I threw my clothes on.

I halted, gauging the boat's distance and counting seconds. 'Me? You made a prediction about me?' Everybody in East Anglia seemed to have been seancing or whatever it's called about me, yet I was the only one who hadn't heard this prediction. 'Out with it, Bea.' I honestly wasn't worried, but I'd got plenty of time so I dawdled. Only from mild interest, honestly.

Bea was so matter-of-fact. She was doing her nails. 'You

are the one who sees, Lovejoy. But you will be blinded by power from the past.' I waited for the punch line, then realized there wasn't any more.

'That it?' I yelped. I was risking my neck, if not more vital parts, by staying listening to this rubbish. 'For Christ's sake, Bea.' I gave her a quick buss for thanks and headed out of her bedroom. The pilot boat was now half way across the harbour, travelling at a hell of a lick. I zoomed on to the landing.

'Just death, Lovejoy,' Bea's voice added.

I stopped and said it all in one. 'Death? Whose?' Still rubbish, of course, because I'm not superstitious. In fact I may be the only non-superstitious bloke left. But where's the harm?'

'A death. Between the salt water and the sea sand.'

That old line again, wasn't it from the ancient song *Scarborough Fayre*? I said airily, 'Not mine, then?'

'That was not revealed.'

'Try harder next time. Tara, love.'

She called after me. 'Lovejoy. Watch that woman. I don't like her. Them Scorpios are all the same.' That was more like it, I thought approvingly. Women's hatreds are to be trusted.

I returned a sentence of merry abuse, opened the door and ran straight into Donna Vernon.

'Lovejoy. He said you'd be here.' She was stiff and white with rage. Tinker was dozing in her car, the old nerk. I went pale—not too difficult to do because Barney was ascending the wharfside's stone steps behind her. He's the size of a house. His hands were like dangling shovels. Probably used them for rowing with.

'Wotcher, Barney, me old hearty,' I chirruped with poisonous good cheer.

'You been seeing Beatrice, Lovejoy?' he rumbled.

'No. We're trying to knock her up, aren't we, Mrs Vernon? There's no answer.' Swiftly I gave Barney a roguish leer before somebody told the truth. 'Maybe she's already up-stairs waiting to say welcome sailor.' Mrs Vernon gave me the age-old look, guessing that nobody had better say anything.

Muttering, Barney heaved his hulk inside, lightening the sky for miles. I knew Beatrice wouldn't reveal all. She has ways of stifling any protest Barnacle Bill could utter. The door slammed behind him, to my relief, good old Donna's signal.

'Lovejoy, you bastard!' she yelled in a ladylike manner.

'Be this your sodding car, mate?' a fisherman called. He had a million boxes of dead silver things. I looked away, queasy. Tinker had nodded off. 'It's in our frigging way.'

'It's all okay, Mrs Vernon,' I wheedled, thinking fast. 'I just had to check you out with Beatrice. It sounded so odd to, er, an unbeliever. I'll come with you. Honestly. And I'll behave. Oh.' I made a theatrical gesture of surprise. 'Hang on. Shall I turn your car? It's so narrow on the wharf . . .' I moved swiftly past her and got in. Beatrice was looking down from her upstairs window, still in her sorcerer's apprentice outfit and smiling down with a silent tut-tut on her lovely mouth. She was about to draw her bedroom curtains now Barney was in situ. Donna Vernon stood waiting, still smarting.

I smiled apologetically to show that everything wasn't my fault, gave Beatrice a papal blessing, and drove off.

CHAPTER 5

There was a list of addresses in the glove compartment which tallied. About five o'clock that same day, me and Tinker drove into Nottingham, top name. He'd been snoring his head off, which was fine by me because I wanted to think about Donna Vernon, seances and vanishing antique-dealer husbands.

And old songs. I wasn't so daft that I hadn't recognized
the line. Everybody knows those Early English riddle mel-
odies. Little girls still do rope-skip chants to them in the
streets, and nowadays pop groups re-compose them for
sordid gain. As if they think we're too thick to notice that
everybody's been singing them for a thousand years. I
hummed *Scarborough Fayre* till I found the stanza:

> 'Tell him to buy me an acre of land,
> Parsley, sage, rosemary and thyme,
> Atwixt the salt water and the sea sand,
> Then he'll be a true love of mine . . .'

The punch line being that there's no land at all between the
ocean and the sand, so the girl singing it thinks the bloke's
a dud lover. As a song it's nowt special, but that haunting
line held a terrible hint of permanence. I shut up singing
and drove.

Nottingham's one of those bright towns, like York and
Lancaster, which look as if even their rain's shinier than
every place else's. I quite took to it. Of course their Council's
battered its priceless architecture into rubble on which
they've built car parks and council offices of staggering
dullness, but that's only par these days. On the outskirts I
stopped and checked Mrs Vernon's walletful of valuable
information, then followed the map. Once, I stopped to
phone. Tinker got on my nerves, keepng on rousing to ask
blearily where we were, as if it mattered to him. It's worse
when he's kipping. He sucks and blows through his few
grotty brown teeth continually. It's a gruesome business
when a bean gets lodged between his fangs. I decided to
ditch him, for a useful purpose of course.

The house was about seven miles out of town in a smallish
place where Nottingham's buses were beginning to worry
about getting back and motors rested in garden driveways
instead of out in the road. For a long minute as the engine

cooled I waited. The garden notice, *St Peter's Rectory*, worried
me, but no good sitting on my bum. After all, there's no
way of judging wars that never start; wars that actually
happen are easy. I had to find which sort of war this rectory
represented.

'Have a zuzz, Tinker. Back in a sec.'

'Right, mate.'

The postage-stamp of lawn, weak-kneed rhododendrons
and the reeling trellis with a back-combed firethorn were
entirely predictable. St Peter himself opened the door. I
admired his massive beard, though to me beards always
look full of dandruff.

'You're Lovejoy, who phoned. Do come in. Thank
heavens you've brought no children.' He wrung my hand.
'They scream.'

'The beard's new, eh?' I guessed, following him in. He
wasn't quite as gnarled as vicars were when I was a lad,
and wore quite a natty grey jacket. 'Nottingham's Oberam-
mergau? Who're you playing?'

He gave an unexpectedly toothy grin. 'You're sharp. I
actually grew it for the village dramatic society. I'm a
murderer. My wife has designs on her sister's fortune. She
makes me stab her lover and poisons her family's banker.'

'Great plot,' I said gravely. He'd brewed up as soon as
I'd phoned and had cups laid on a tea-tray. The living-room
was a small cube crammed with modern furniture-shaped
gunge. My eyes tried to stay away from the cardboard shoe
box on the mantelpiece where a Victorian pop-up card
rested in calm superiority. That little card was slumming,
and knew it. 'I expected an antique shop, actually, er,
Reverend.'

'Call me Joe,' he said, passing me a cup. 'When you rang
I was just on my way to rehearsal, so I'm afraid . . .'

'I'll only be a minute. An antique dealer called recently,
didn't he, er, Joe? Mr Vernon.'

'Ah yes. Nothing wrong, I hope? He was very disappointed the aigrette had been sold—I think that's what they're called. One of our ladies bought it before he arrived.'

Aigrette. So Hubby Vernon was real, had been here, and had been right to be disappointed. An aigrette is a hat-brooch, usually eighteenth-century, shaped so as to hold a feather, and made of gold or silver. Often they themselves were feather-shaped—an egret is some sort of bird—or fashioned as a spray of wayside flowers. I felt relieved. The trail was no longer imaginary. 'It had little stones in it, though I'm afraid it was coming loose.'

I suddenly felt ill. 'You mean part of it wobbled?'

'Mmmh,' he said. His beard wobbled sympathetically in sorrow. 'I tried to fix it but there was some spring thing inside. I reduced the price, of course,' he added hurriedly, in case I got the wrong idea. 'You don't think nine pounds too much, Lovejoy? It was really very pretty.'

The stupid old bastard. I could have strangled him. Let's hope the stage crew got carried away and did away with the moron at tonight's dress rehearsal, for the *tremblant* type of aigrette is rarest of all. It's cleverly made to quiver with every toss of a fair lady's head, thereby setting the jewels flashing and attracting amorous admiration away from less expensively dressed rivals.

'No,' I said, choking, keeping control. 'Nine quid's really quite fair.' Whoever owned it could now pay off that trouble-some mortgage and still offer crumpets for tea. His anxiety evaporated in a grin, silly loon.

'I trust Mr Vernon isn't in any trouble?'

'None. I'm just trying to find him, you see. An urgent family matter. I'm in the trade, chancing to be nearby.'

He tutted. 'I'm afraid he was only one of a hundred or so people who came to the sale. We don't normally—' his eyes twinkled good-humouredly in the undergrowth of his hairy halo '—enter the market place, Lovejoy!'

Faintly I moaned, 'A jumble?' Everybody else flukes a fortune except me.

'We prefer to call it a bring-and-buy,' Joe said primly. 'Emphasizes the role of the providers.'

'Did he come specifically for the aigrette?'

'No. As far as I can remember he just asked our organizer if the best brooch had been sold. My wife Janice said she was sorry but it had—she's our secretary. We chatted a little because he wasn't one of our own flock. He didn't really seem very interested in our wares.'

'Best brooch?' Funny phrase, I thought. And funnier behaviour from a bloke doing an antiques sweep. We have a saying in this lunatic game of madness and money: one look's never enough. Yet here was a geezer who couldn't even bother to walk round a church hall where any of a dozen stalls could hold yet another Koh-i-noor diamond. I rose to go, smiling thanks, and still pretending not to notice the Victorian pop-up card.

'I don't suppose you have any items left over, Joe? Just in case somebody's missed a Rembrandt by mistake.'

'Ah, you dealers!' He laughed, waggled a roguish finger. 'There's only the remnants. Like that box of old cards.'

Casually I stepped across and gave as convincing a chuckle as I could manage.

'Why, it's a Victorian greeting-card!' I said, delighted. 'My old Gran's got a boxful at home too.' The one on display showed a little girl carrying a red heart, sitting on a coloured tissue-paper airship. Fold it, and it would flatten for posting. The card was worth anybody's weekly wage. Some are even dearer. As well as pop-ups you get 'sliders'—push a protruding tab and the scene changes from, say, a nursery of prancing infants to a snowy scene of lakes and sledges.

'That's the best of them,' Joe confessed. 'The others are just old Valentines and things.'

I turned jokingly to him. 'All right, Joe. I'll take them off your hands, as a contribution to your church and its murderous drama. Don't show me what there is inside the box. Come on, drive a hard bargain now!'

Grinning with toothy shyness, he extorted a couple of notes from me. I chucked in a quid extra to obviate any comeback if he ever discovered their true value, and took my leave with the shoe box under my arm. I was elated, because I was suddenly wealthier than I'd been for a long time. Too much to hope for a Horsley original, the very first Christmas card—Sir Henry Cole began it all in that chilly December of 1843 when he discovered himself embarrassingly late with his Christmas letters and got his pal John Horsley to design a jolly printed card, bless them both. Horsley only printed a thousand, but still there might be an 1848 Egley card, the first with holly and mistletoe.

In the car Tinker was coughing himself awake, the car trembling at the unleashed bronchitic energy. I guessed it must be around opening time. 'Where to now, Lovejoy?'

'A nice quiet pub. I've a boxful of old cards to look at.'

The old duck-egg gave a snort of derision at my pleasure. I drove us off reflecting on the differences in people. Tinker really can't see the point in actually loving antiques. I can't see the point in loving anything else.

That evening I'll remember for a long time, with Tinker reminiscing about antique auctions and swilling ale, and me divvying through a glorious collection of old hearts-and-flowers.

I'd won thirty-odd Valentines, a few World War I postcards, and several early Christmas cards. Tip: never pass a box of rubbishy old tat. There's one outside every old junkshop. Remember that Queen Victoria sent over 2,500 Valentines with her very own lilywhites. On the law of averages alone any one dusty old heap of dog-eared cards will conceal a small fortune. The card-sending habit's fairly new, but Valentine wishes in the form of letters or poems goes back much further—naturally, since Henry VIII established Valentine's Day by Royal charter in the 1530s, naughty old devil.

Nottingham's taverns did us proud that night for hot grub. Going on for ten o'clock I carelessly put the motor in the central car park and gave Tinker my last notes for a dosshouse somewhere. By then I'd found a pub whose landlord had a brother who was an antique dealer. We did a 'provo'—a firm deal with prices agreed but provisional on condition of the items sold. I kept ten mixed cards enveloped up for myself. The landlord's brother, one Josh Thompson, would join me at breakfast to close the deal.

There was no way I could contact Lydia but I rang Margaret to pass a message on to say I was okay. Dangerous territory, using women as go-betweens, so I was carefully noncommittal about what I was doing and where I was.

That night I settled down determined to sleep the sleep of the just, but Vernon's weird term kept coming to mind: 'the best brooch'. Who on earth uses words like that, for heaven's sake? As if Vernon was making up some description, not really looking for anything in particular. Yet there was the precise address in what was presumably Donna Vernon's own handwriting, and Reverend Joe's name, J. Cunliffe, Rd. The sort of curt abbreviation you often see in local newspaper ads. Aha. Another clue.

Mystery: Antique-Dealer Sidney Vernon launches a sweep looking for antiques, respectably enough. He zooms off with a list of contacts, yet doesn't get heartburn when missing a luscious antique by a whisker, and doesn't even bother to suss out the rest of the stuff on sale. Really weird.

Despite all, I eventually slept like a log and was downstairs whistling for breakfast by seven-thirty. Seeing Donna Vernon drinking coffee in the pub lounge, while motherly women vacuumed the carpets and shook dusters from leaded windows, brought me down to earth.

CHAPTER 6

' 'Morning, Lovejoy,' La Vernon said, simultaneously calm and furious. Women have the knack of being both, which is why we live in a woman's world.

' 'Morning, Mrs Vernon.'

She held out her hand. I dropped her car keys into the palm and sat. I'd been stupid to assume that she'd not follow. Evading police is easy. Escaping a woman isn't. Now why, I wondered as a bright lady came to serve, did she need me along? Hiring me made less and less sense. Nobody in his right mind would believe she was guided to me by Bea's tea-leaf gazing and that seance rubbish.

'Good morning, sir. What would you like for breakfast?'

I stared at the lady. Sometimes I honestly don't believe what I'm hearing. 'I'd like breakfast for breakfast, please.'

The woman laughed, pinking. She was chained to a notepad. Cold buzzie and cold feet but warm heart, I knew instantly, because this sort always has. 'No. Do you want continental breakfast, or—?'

'Forgotten what your granny taught you, love? Breakfast is eggs and bacon and toast and marmalade, and porridge if mice haven't dumped in the oats.'

'We've no time,' Mrs Vernon rasped.

'See you around then, Donna,' I said politely. 'Get a move on, missus. I'm bloody starving.'

The cleaning women were having a good laugh but keeping a weather eye on my unexpected visitor.

'Don't tell me, boss,' I guessed resignedly. 'You got the train to Nottingham, taxied round, spotted your crate, then asked at the nearest pub for somebody answering my description, right?'

'Quicker than that, Lovejoy.' She lit a cigarette, which I

extinguished in her coffee. She instantly erupted. 'What the—?'

'There's a William IV hunting-scene on the panelling behind you, love,' I told her. 'Your fag's bad for its chest.' Might as well talk to the wall. She still glared. 'Look. Hadn't you best just give me a photograph of your husband, then get out of my way?'

She didn't know which to be maddest at, me, her drenched fag, or being told to get lost. 'But I hired you, Lovejoy! You're supposed to do what I want!'

The world's full of incompetents crying that tale. 'Oh, aye,' I said unbelievingly and waded into my porridge which arrived just in time to save me fainting. I eat it as it comes. Milk makes scarey patterns and sugar makes oats see-through. An old colonel and his missus were having Douglas kippers in the corner, with toast thin as rice-paper. They wouldn't get far on that.

'Let's get one thing clear, Lovejoy,' Mrs Vernon ground out. 'Your sexist attitude's a propaganda put-down, Lovejoy. It's oppressionism. It's totalitarianism. You default on me and I'll—'

'Sue me? It'll take ten lawyers a costly year and I'm broke. I'm fed up with you.'

She eyed me. Slowly, almost with an audible click, her brain began to function. Sooner or later it always happens, though oftentimes too late. 'So it's you go on your own, Lovejoy?'

'Why not? I'm unemployed.' I couldn't resist putting that nasty bit in. 'I've got the list of places where he's gone.'

'Because I . . .' She paused, made to reach for her coffee, changed her mind when seeing her fag bobbing in the caffeine.

'See?' I said gently. 'Your hiring me, all that rigmarole about mediums, stars, crystal balls, Owd Maggie's dream-time. It was nonsense.'

'Tell me why,' she said, looking. Her eyes were blue,

fetchingly done with eyebrows all her own and eyelashes a foot long. If only she had Edwardian stud-and-drop earrings or something, or even those modern multicoloured titanium surfacers, and a ton more make-up, she'd look . . . no, she wouldn't. It wasn't just that she was everything Lydia wasn't. There was something else. A shut-out, a mental armour. It was in her. Thank God most women are her opposite.

'Give my acquaintance a fresh cup, wench,' I said to the lady who was busy shovelling eggs, bacon, beans and sausages in front of me. 'She's been a dirty girl with that one. But don't put it on my bill or I'll never get rid of her. And why?' I continued to Mrs Vernon. 'Because you could have simply phoned around and asked how far your husband had got. Or come after him on your tod.'

'Tod?'

'Tod Malone, own. You could have done this without me. You're a resourceful lass.' An overcoated bloke came in, chatted to the cleaners and glanced over to me. He seemed quite at home. Us antique dealers are like those countries which once belonged to the same empire—competitors, but united for eternity from a shared belief in the same myth. It's not just the lingo. You can tell an antique dealer a mile off.

'I've explained all that.' She was quite cool. 'I need a divvie. My husband has our entire savings. We're at a critical time in our relationship. He's . . . not a very practical man. And a belief in the occult is not a crime. The only warning against you is that you are not to be trusted. But who is?'

Indeed. Good old Cardew wasn't so dumb.

'Whose side am I on? Hubby's or yours?' I was beginning to sound like a hireling.

She drank her scalding coffee. How women can do that beats me. My tea passes the elbow test before I can even sip on the rim. I noshed gamely on, waiting for more orders, like I'd done once for shellfire.

She rose. 'How soon can you be ready, Lovejoy?' She almost choked on the mildness of it. The overcoated bloke had strolled into the kitchen, a publican's antique-dealing brother if ever I saw one.

'Half an hour to finish. I've someone to see first.' Going red, I added, 'Please,' and watched her recede across the carpeted lounge. The attractive serf bringing the toast— proper slices, not like the colonel's thin triangles with no edges—watched her too. And the cleaners, and the colonel and his missus. Mrs Vernon was watchable and obeyable, but probably not much else.

'What do you reckon, love?' I asked, lashing out with the marmalade.

'I wouldn't like to get on the wrong side of her,' the lady confided frankly, busily rearranging the pots.

'It is hell,' I agreed. 'Incidentally, tell that bloke you've dragged into your lair that the greatest antique dealer in the known world is now prepared to receive him.'

'You saucy devil. And I can't say I took to her friend, either.'

My marmalade hand froze. 'Friend?'

'Looked a right misery.' The description she gave—pale, thirtyish, wary—matched up to the bloke from the seance. The one I'd felt watching me sideways. He'd apparently arrived with Donna Vernon, carefully leaving before I'd come down.

Well, I told myself nervously after a think, there's no law against it, is there?

Josh Thompson turned out to be one of those friendly utility models, no time-waster. A brisk slogger without flair, but a stayer who'd be making a good living from this delirious antiques game when much cleverer blokes have died the Icarus death of over-ambition. I liked him. We did a good deal for the bulk of the cards, me chopping the mark-up for cash (translation: taking only half profit, for filthy lucre on the spot). I paid for his coffee, big spender me, and the greedy sod nicked four slices of my toast. I felt I could trust him, so didn't and asked him about three of the nearest people listed on Mrs Vernon's paper. He knew two, and spoke of them with Nottinghamshire bluntness and at great length. I was delighted at the progress I was making.

Like I say, a born duck-egg.

I've met some vengeful women in my time, but this one wasn't so direct as the others. There was a reserve, something held back. She felt emotionally wrong. I tried warning myself off because I'd got enough trouble to be going on with, and anyway antiques are a full-time love. It's well known that love affairs should come one at a time.

Anyhow, right or wrong, I was becoming quite interested in Mrs Vernon. I couldn't help watching her as we drove away: confident, sharp, aggressive. The weather promised warm and the dress she wore had a pale green self-stripe, some silk material that caught the light. She drove intently, slightly hunched, casting frequent glances at the rearview mirror and rolling the steering-wheel like rally drivers do.

But even she, expert driver as she was, had a hell of a time getting us out of Nottingham. Like most ancient places its traffic now follows guess-where merry-go-rounds until good luck reprieves it and you blunder out down some side street. I was sorry to be leaving, though. I would miss the smiles and the antiques, but not Tinker. Unless the booze had hit hard he would soon be shuffling into the pub where I'd stayed. There he would find my letter and the gelt to follow at his speediest, which is small in velocity but certain. He never questions orders wrapped in money.

'Is this the time to ask about you?' I tried.

'No,' I got back.

'Hubby, then?'

Her pause wasn't indecision. More for effect, to show she was still calling the tune. Then she began to explain as we made it from the inner maze and bowled towards our next joint triumph.

She had met Sid Vernon while she was a secretary for a London auction firm near Hanover Square when he had called to arrange the sale of a painting, a lovely Northcote oil of a lady.

'Not Sir Joshua Reynold's missus?' I cracked, smiling.

She did not respond, which puzzled me, and sailed on: 'Sid and I married. He set up business near Hampstead. I did the documentation, he the antiques. We recently moved out of London, sold the house, cheaper district, that sort of thing. Lately Sid planned to do a sweep through East Anglia because paintings are our thing, and there's nowhere like it for finding genuine Old Masters, is there? He drew our capital and left about three weeks ago. His sweep was going to take a fortnight.'

'You've not heard since?'

'Not directly. It was drawn out as a money order.'

Movable anywhere in the Kingdom, and untraceable. Clever old Sid.

'And the seance bit?'

'It's a sensible precaution to take the best advice, Lovejoy. You're just stupid.'

Well, yes, but not so stupid as a bird who calls assorted English paintings 'Old Masters', and who doesn't know that the great Reynolds had as weird a bunch of pupils and followers as you could ever imagine. The point is that James Northcote studied under Sir Joshua, and wrote the great man's biography. Ostensibly full of praise, it has become the alltime classic backhander, packed with the cleverest malice you'll ever come across. Read it and see for yourself. The book's a collector's item. A couple of fascinating but odious blokes. I remember one unsigned Reynolds School

portrait which me and Rex from Polstead faked and sold in
Suffolk—

'Lovejoy?'

'Er, yes, I quite agree,' I replied hurriedly We were
bowling along and signs saying Lincoln were starting to
appear. Hers was a good story, for a pack of lies. Other
people's falsehoods always make me switch off.

She took us to a roadhouse where we freshened up and
had a snack. Then we hurried into Lincoln while our state
of truce lasted.

Exactly then I realized that the last person she wanted
back in bed was good old Sid, because I was almost sure
there was a thin, pale, wary-faced bloke in a Mini waiting
at the traffic lights as Donna thrust a map at me and
demanded directions. Different story now, I observed, and
a different type of pursuit. Circumstances alter chases. I
avoided staring in the bloke's direction and concentrated on
the chart. Odd coincidence that we see him here. Maybe he
was on the way to another seance?

CHAPTER 7

'This it?'

Following the map we found a street of small terraced
houses. A push-chair leaned folded against the wall. A
plastic toy was up-ended nearby, and a child's tricycle lay
in the gutter. The rest of Lincoln is beautiful. I'd drawn the
short straw.

'It must be, Lovejoy. Stay here.'

'Like hell.' I was out and knocking before she could reply.

The woman who came to the door carried a bulbous
infant and had the hunted look that comes from struggle.
A tatty little girl sucked two thumbs behind her mother's
skirt.

'Hello, love. Mrs E. Smith? I'm trying to catch Mr Vernon. He called a while since.'

She had been pretty once. Now dishevelled and harassed, she still had some of that allure simply because all women keep it no matter what. Her presentation was just a little awry.

'Who?'

'Listen, lady,' Mrs Vernon began, but I deliberately stepped in front of her.

'My secretary will wait in the car,' I said cheerfully. The bulbous cherub had gone red and was grunting. I took it and pushed gently inside the corridor. God, it was heavy.

'He's got George,' the little girl pointed out.

Vaguely I wondered if infants are made of denser stuff. Maybe they don't use lead-free petrol in Lincoln and it gets in their little bones. Skilfully I hoofed the door shut in Donna's apoplectic face and just made it to the shambolic living-room before collapsing under George's weight.

The mother followed wearily, not a peep out of her. She looked all in. I might have been the gas man. Her house had everything: peeling paint, begrimed walls, shredding wallpaper child-picked into lakes of bare plaster, and an antique hanging on the wall that made my chest go *boing*. With difficulty I ignored it, breathing hard. George gaped at me without affection, masticating a dummy tit and grunting pinkly. Down in the forest something stirred. I was being dumped on.

'Sit down, chuck,' I told the woman, undoing the babe and honestly gazing at the little girl instead of the Russian amber rosary beads hanging from a nail on the wall though my eyes wavered like a hunter's. 'My name's Lovejoy. Where's his nappy?'

The little girl went to a cupboard for a folded nappy. She leant her elbows on my knee, watching. The mother couldn't have been more than twenty-four. She observed listlessly, hands clasped between her knees dragging her frock tight. Talk about washed out.

I explained to the little girl, 'Men have no laps, see? We use chairs, but you can do it on the floor.'

She nodded, swinging a foot, understanding life's defects. Changing the cherub was like dressing a wriggling bolster. George was melodious, bawling a lusty barcarole while I got a bowl and washed his bum. Skilfully he peed a squirt into the clean nappy. 'A born critic you've got here, chuck,' I said to the woman. She nodded, not a smile. I salted him with talcum and propped him upright while he sang on. He nearly had half a tooth.

'There!' Difficult to keep calm with my chest chiming like a cathedral gone berserk. That luscious rosary was genuine and old.

Gedanite's a pine resin which ages into a false amber. It's usually opaque yellow and so brittle it's hell to work. But whoever had cut this rosary had been a master craftsman. Each bead was engraved with Christian symbols and the crucifix was ecstatic. 'Clean as a new pin, Elsie, Elisabeth? Where's your bloke?'

'Ellen. Gone,' she said, almost smiling at the monster. He was now standing doing the infant's painful trick of marching on my thighs.

'That his rosary?'

'No. Mine,' she said, shrugging. 'I run a business, home hairdressing, in the next room. It's not much. So I tried . . . '

'Selling it?' I prompted gently. My mini-Tarzan was yodelling, stamping, bellowing his tuneless song and dribbling a length of elasticated grot which pendulated from his half-tooth. They're a puzzle. If I'd just dried him, why were we now both drenched?

'He wasn't interested.'

'Where did you advertise?'

'*Advertiser*. An advert's free, you see.'

'He didn't sweep you off your feet?' It was a joke. She shook her head in all seriousness.

'He was in a hurry. Nobody else came.' Her eyes focused on me for the first time. 'My grandma said it was special, but I suppose fashions change, don't they?' She desperately wanted something constant in the oppressive poverty-stricken world she had somehow come to inhabit.

'Too often,' I lied. 'Here, did you say you were a hair-dresser?'

'I can't do perms . . .'

'Good heavens,' I said enthusiastically. 'My secretary needs her hair doing.'

'She does? But the shopping . . .'

'Please. Her hair's a mess.' Be firm, Lovejoy. 'I'll shop for you. Has this thing been fed?'

'He eats all the time,' she explained listlessly. 'Marilyn knows the way.'

I raised my voice to carry over the syncopating songster now churning my thighbones to powder. 'Then shout her in and give me his campaign rations.'

A minute later I explained my plan to Donna Vernon. 'Mrs E. Smith will do your hair,' I said calmly.

'She'll what?'

'I'll be gone an hour. I'm furthering your interests.' While Donna Vernon did her nut I swept out, humping George and dragging Marilyn. We slung the rickety push-chair into the car boot and took off for Lincoln's busy centre.

'You're neck's wet. It's our George's spit,' Marilyn pointed out.

'I noticed.' I was knee-deep in it.

'Why've we stolen Grandma's beads, Lovejoy?'

There was a momentary silence while I reversed into the car park. The eagle-eyed little pest must have spotted me. While loading us up I'd torn a piece of my jacket lining away to wrap it in, with secret skill.

'We haven't exactly nicked them,' I explained. 'Mummy couldn't sell them. So we're going to, see?'

'Mummy says nobody'll buy them beads, Lovejoy.'

See how even miniature women focus on gelt? 'Mummys are usually wrong,' I pronounced. The heresy worked. She gave an awed gasp. It was in a temporary lull that we disembarked.

George's push-chair was so warped it looked semi-melted, something painted by Dali. Marilyn did his straps while I transferred the 'Disabled' sticker from a nearby car to ours. Nothing wrong with this little deception. Other deceivers were thronging into the precinct: the saloon racers with phoney I'm-allowed stickers, the council-clerks' Daimlers with exemption pennants, off-duty policemen whose black-mail is subtler than most. Law's enough to make a cat laugh.

We set off. The damned push-chair had a wonky wheel. What with that, my irritating wet collar, George's incessant crooning and Marilyn telling other shoppers we'd stolen Grandma's beads, I was in a state by the time we'd done the shopping. When I finally crack it won't be from World War Three. It'll be queuing at the checkout where the till girl runs out of change and all your goods come funnelling at you too fast into your wheelie and the queue's exasperated because you're holding everybody up and you've paid nearly a quid for one measly ragged lettuce. I nearly went mental that morning, but little Marilyn was great. She caught our stuff like an Australian fielder and rebuilt the pyramidal display of dogfood tins which George had shambled by removing the keystone can as we hurtled past, so I was a knackered wreck when we finally hit the street and found a miraculously unvandalized telephone. Margaret Dainty was in and phoned me back within five minutes with the ad-dresses I wanted.

'What's that noise, Lovejoy?' Margaret wanted to know as I scribbled them down.

'Do me a favour and phone Michaela French. She seems nearest to where I am.' We were by the lovely house locals call the Cardinal's Hat—though Cardinal Wolsey didn't need his hat for long—so it would mean a plod up Hungate,

Michaelgate and beyond. 'Tell her I'll be round.'

'Watch her, Lovejoy. I see her at the antique fairs. A cool customer. Hates paying a price. What *is* that wailing?'

'A singing baby,' I said irritably.

'Did you say a singing . . .?'

Michaela French's antique shop was disturbingly much posher than I'd hoped. It stood in a small tangle of mediæval streets on a hell of a slope. I loved the vibes, even exhausted as I was from shoving George's inert mass uphill. Lincoln's somehow managed to defend itself against architects. Pleased at the sight of the castle and the rich feeling from the ancient stones, I resolved to be especially charming to Michaela French while I sold her my—well, Grandma's— genuine Russian rosary.

'You're in charge of George, Marilyn,' I said, threatening fire and slaughter if she moved an inch and warning that I'd be watching through the shop window.

'Are you going to leave us?' Marilyn asked.

Children are a right nuisance. I looked at her. 'No,' I said. 'I've changed my mind.' Anyway I'd only have been on tenterhooks, wondering if I'd remembered to put the brake on the bloody push-chair. 'Come on.'

Michaela French was as trendy as her name. She was showing a wide-banded ring to a nice elderly couple. They were impressed. So was I, but in a different way. Nearly thirty, slender, dark, shapely, dressed with that costly beige sloppiness you only see where they own the nextdoor's freehold and have coffee and cake brought in for elevenses. She was at the orgasm point of making a sale.

'That reflection deep inside the gemstone,' she was pontificating as we trundled in, 'is proof of a true moonstone. It's known as chatoyancy—yes?' Her hand froze in mid-air, the ring shining in the Anglepoise lamp she'd arranged to conceal the fraud. She eyed George and Marilyn and me, in that order.

'I'll wait.' My endearing grin didn't work.

'I don't buy in from the street,' she said to me, smiling apology at the couple.

'Very wise,' I said affably.

Clearly I was expected to go. I waited. George bellowed another verse and broke wind with spectacular shrillness. Marilyn swung a leg and gazed with dispassion at Michaela French, who now wanted scalps.

'Could you please leave?' she said sharply. She laughed gaily at the customers. 'Some people don't realize we're rather above the usual run of antique businesses.'

We could try somewhere else. I got the door open as she resumed her spiel: 'It is early Venetian, of course. These Jewish marriage rings often have a canopy; the simpler ones are true sixteenth-century. The others are imitation.'

'Have we to go?' Marilyn asked.

Marilyn had a peculiarly flat way of stating questions that was starting to nark me. In fact her questions weren't really questions at all. They were assertions, and they all said the same thing: *It's always too good to be true*. She only came up to my knee. Practically still a sprog, and a pessimist. The whole world suddenly went red. I thought: Bugger this for a lark.

Michaela French nattered on, having dismissed the riff-raff. 'The bride wore the ring for life . . .'

'No, chuck,' I said loudly to Marilyn. 'Let's stay, eh?'

I hauled us over to a re-covered chaise-longue. La French did her freeze. I mouthed a smiling, 'I'll wait' to her and sat me and Marilyn. George boomed a bellyful of melody into a hostile universe.

'I'm so sorry. One moment, please.'

Michaela French dabbed at a digital phone and muttered discreetly into it, clattered it home. The peelers were coming. Heyho.

'She's told on us,' Marilyn whispered.

'Then we'll tell on her.' I said it loud enough to hear down in Mint Lane.

'They were always Venetian,' Michaela French angrily resumed. Her breathing had gone funny. 'And gold—'

'Fakes,' I announced innocently, 'are common, Marilyn. See that picture frame? The one marked 'genuine'? They build it up using mashed parchment in whiting powder and glovers' leather scraps boiled into jelly. They spread the *gesso* lovely and level, maybe nine or ten coats. Phoney.'

There was silence all around. George parped and whistled. God knows what his mother fed him. He sounded like a sink constantly emptying.

'They put vermilion in the gilding.' I spoke over George's bagpipe belly. 'Look at it sideways and you'll see where the old crevices have been done with modern gilding. Old frame-makers only did that where their agate burnisher tool couldn't touch. Part of that frame's not genuine at all.'

Marilyn nodded, sucking her thumbs. I made my hands into birds which hovered and dived to throttle George while Marilyn blotted his chin with his bib. He fell about at the bird game, cackling as Michaela French, white and murderous, spoke determinedly on: 'The Jewish marriage ring invariably has a light feel—'

'Similor's lightweight, love,' I told Marilyn. 'Cheap old alloy. French bloke called Renty invented it: *similar* to *or*, gold. Get it?' I chuckled, eyeing the ceiling reminiscently. 'You can't teach the French anything about forging jewellery. They're great. Do a hell of a trade faking "specials"—like Continental Jewish rings. Of course,' I went on conversationally, 'good forgery's cheap. They used any old stuff for gemstones. Grotty bits of waste quartz, for instance. Like the nice lady's got there.'

A man outside was looking at the shop. Even without the uniformed bobby with him he spelled the Old Bill.

'These rings are very rare items,' Michaela French rasped furiously to her now apprehensive customers.

'You see, Marilyn,' I coursed on, 'it gives a chatoyancy reflection. But so do plenty of other stones. Fakers always use it, copying tourmaline, chrysoberyl, moonstone . . .'

George squawked irritably so I resumed the bird game as the peelers came in. The tourists sidestepped, smiling anxious smiles, out of the door.

The plainclothes man stood, cleared his throat, rocked on his heels. Why *do* they do that? 'Good morning, lady. You reported a disturbance?'

'Yes. This man here . . .'

Benignly I looked up, smiling my most innocent smile at the ring she still held. Threats rarely work but it's all you can do when a woman's lecturing the world on her rights.

'Yes?' The man was between me and the door. The bobby stood nearby staring at the woman's shape.

She started again. 'This scruff . . .' And paused. I'd explained her transparent fraud to two gullible tourists. I could just as easily explain it to the Old Bill. And their Antiques Squad down by St James's in London have interesting ways of proving if you're right. Or, even, wrong. Being one goal up's a novel feeling. I liked it. I smiled at everyone.

'Name?' the Old Bill said.

'Lovejoy.'

Michaela French stared. A lot of readjustment was going on. Margaret had phoned after all. She was trying to equate this infant-toting yob with the divvie she had heard of.

I helped her. 'My, er, colleague phoned, I trust?'

'Thank you for coming,' she said with difficulty, then started inventing. 'Er, yes, Inspector. Lovejoy arrived as I was having rather a little problem with some customers. He was, ah, very kind. He offered to stay until, ah, you arrived.'

'I see.'

The burly man was unsatisfied. There was note-taking and form-signing before they left. I was beginning to feel ill-used. Whose fault was all this? Not mine, nor Marilyn's. We were only here for the beer, so to speak, and already we were surrounded by peelers. No wonder you get narked.

I'm always the baddie in the last bloody reel.

We waved the Old Bill goodbye. George fluted a gaseous farewell of his own composition.

Alone.

Michaela French cupped her elbows, fingers tapping. 'You're not what I expected, Lovejoy.' I shrugged. It's not my fault that I'm a disappointment.

'Michaela, may I introduce Miss Marilyn Smith, spinster of this parish, and George Smith, bass-baritone.' George's rotund belly lessened with an audible parp. Me and Marilyn leaned away from the niff. 'Pardon,' I said for him. 'I have a Russian-carved rosary.' I pulled it out, undid it.

'Lovejoy ripped his coat to wrap Grandma's beads in,' Marilyn explained. 'We pinched them. His mummy'll smack.'

Michaela sat, looking at me. 'Oh, did he?'

'Shut it, you,' I told Marilyn, 'or we'll never reach the border. It's gedanite, not true amber. Gdansk.' I held the rosary, moved almost to tears. Even in its encrustation of grime and dust it glowed with a matt radiance you don't often see. 'The trouble is women spray themselves with deodorants and perfumes. They never think to protect their amber jewellery. Ambers and near-ambers like this run a terrible risk from solvents.'

She was sitting quietly. 'And this hasn't?'

'No,' I said delightedly. 'It's only ever been worn outside a man's garments or a priest's cassock.' I frowned, adjusted the light. 'There's a slight chip out of one of the paternoster beads, but all the ave marias are mint. And the crucifix. Needs cleaning and feeding, but do you ever find amber that doesn't nowadays?'

'Can the chip be mended?'

'With your eyes closed.' I shoved her rubbishy ring and papers aside and snaked the rosary to show off its five exquisite decades of beads. The six larger paternoster beads were carved with microscopic scenes and Russian lettering.

The solemn cross was perfection. 'I've only seen one of these before. It wasn't a patch on this.'

'How old is it, Lovejoy?'

'The gedanite's fifty million years, give or take a week. The carving's 1810.' Whoever had carved it had done the world a favour. In the gaud paternoster carving you could actually see crowds clustering about the streets. 'I once tried carving a scrap of gedanite and finished up with a heap of flakes. It's murder. The old carvers must have had some way of softening it that we've lost nowadays, though an old amber bloke once told me warm it in your mouth and it carves like a dream—'

'Is it yours to sell?'

'Cross my heart.'

'And hope to die?' she capped, underhand.

I smiled properly from relief and we got down to it. Margaret Dainty was right. I had a hell of a time even getting her over two hundred, but finally she promised double price once it was authenticated by some amateur crummy London museum like the Victoria and Albert. Bloody cheek.

'And you mend it before you leave, Lovejoy.'

I sighed and took off my jacket. 'Got a fresh sliced loaf?'

Michaela hesitated. It was probably her very first-ever hesitation, so I waited respectfully while this emotional virginity terminated. 'If you three are hungry there's a café . . .' she said.

'Glad to hear it, love,' I said. 'So bring a couple of pasties as well, please.'

Less than an hour later me and Marilyn were noshing in the café. She was feeding semolina to her new doll while I fought George for the last pasty. We'd had three, some chips, eggs and a lot of tomato sauce. The little swine was a bit of a mess from squeezing fistfuls of beans, but I've found that's the trouble with people his age. No control over their desires. The counter-women were laughing and calling encouragement, which is all very well. Women admire appetites, but it's only a device to conceal their indelible crime, the fake promise of deliverance.

Curiously, Michaela French joined us after her second-ever hesitation. She kept well away from George.

'You have to shove the plates out of his reach,' I explained as George flailed the table hunting fistfuls.

'So I see.' She was inclining off at an angle. 'I, ah, wanted to, ah, ask how I treat the chipped bead now.'

'Do nothing. Just don't let anybody brine test it.' I'd told her all this once. In strong brines ambers float. Plastics and cunning fakes usually don't, but the joins loosen.

'I'd never seen that bread trick.'

Mending amber—or virtually any non-metal antique—by bread is absurdly simple. Or cheese, or sour milk. Why people will bother with modern resins I'll never know. There's more on your larder shelf than is dreamt of, etcetera.

'Old English farmhouse sculpture,' I said. 'It became London trinketry, three centuries back. All sorts of varnishes and lacquers—' I paused, breathlessly ramming a bolus of pasty at George's mouth and got a bit myself in the blissful pause— 'for making jewellery. Half the lightweight antique ornamentation around's nothing more than bread. Cheapest way of faking jet. I use nail varnish, spit and paintbox colouring like you saw me. Depends on what you're mending. Or forging,' I added. She remembered the fake antique marriage ring and reddened. It was becoming a day of all-time firsts for Michaela. Hesitation *and* a blush. Whatever next?

While she documented the purchase I'd made a minute pair of floral earrings for Marilyn out of George's miraculously plentiful saliva and bread, and coloured them pale blue with ink before nail-varnishing them. Bread jewellery's lovely, a lost art. It deserves rediscovery. Marilyn wore her

roses proudly on gold sleepers which Michaela surprisingly
chucked in at the last minute.

The deal had been part cash. I'd bought George a white
hat he liked and some woolly shoes but already he had slung
one.

Marilyn's eyes narrowed. 'Your mummy, Lovejoy.'

Not quite. There stood Donna. She was not breathing
quickly but her nostrils showed her lungs only wanted half
a chance. Our party was over.

'Your hair looks nice,' I said hopefully through the last
bit of grub. George squealed exasperation. He'd seen me,
greedy little sod.

'It's still the same, Lovejoy. And it's time we were leaving.' She must have phoned Lydia, who must have guessed
right, that I'd got the addresses of some Lincoln dealers
through Margaret. Irritating to realize that friends know
me so well.

'One second, please,' Michaela said.

'*Now*,' Donna Vernon cut into the icy stillness. I rose,
defeated.

'Tara, George.' I gave Michaela our reserve custard for
the homeward run. 'Watch his spit, love.' It took a second
to scribble my name to endorse Michaela's cheque. 'Give
that to their mother, okay?'

I tried to find a dry spot on George's face, shrugged and
bussed his head. Marilyn was easier and cleaner. She took
the opportunity of whispering in a stage yell, 'I won't tell
about you tearing your jacket, Lovejoy.'

'Great. Tara, Michaela.'

'You promised to ring, Lovejoy,' said Michaela.

'Right,' I said. I'd done no such thing, but what's a
promise between friends?

'We stole Grandma's beads,' Marilyn was proudly telling
people on the next table as I departed with Donna. 'George
spit on Lovejoy's neck.' Michaela looked aghast at being
left in charge. All in all it had been a big day for her.

'Pity we're leaving Lincoln so soon,' I said to Donna. 'Cardew's from here. We could have called.'

Donna said nothing, just drove us on south to Lowestoft. I was uneasy, because Lincoln had proved that Husband Sid could have easily sold Grandma's rosary, just like I'd done. He hadn't. Instead, he'd paid a token call on Mrs Smith and hurried on his way. He'd simply marked the trail.

On the way my whimsical journey lost its mildness. The police suddenly promoted me suspect.

CHAPTER 8

Donna had played hell for a few tight-lipped miles. I said women talk too much. It only got her madder. 'It's true,' I said to explain. 'Most women want to talk even in bed.'

She fixed me with a wintry glare. 'Oh?'

From then on I got the whole silent-screen reproach bit. It was so unnerving that I dropped off. Good pasties in Lincoln. Michaela had been quite attractive at the finish. Pity we'd got off to such a poor start. Maybe if I wasn't such a scruff . . .

A hand shook me awake. 'Would you step outside please, sir?' a policeman was asking. A wah-wah car's blue light was spinning nearby. We were in a lay-by with overtaking traffic slowing while inquisitive drivers peered out at the scene.

Donna ranted and I blearily blustered, but we were taken in just the same. The extra bobby drove our car into the police yard of a smallish rural town I'd never heard of. I think we were now well into East Anglia, but smallish or not it had enough Old Bill to make me feel isolated. A bushy ginger-haired plainclothesman looked through me.

'I'm Sergeant Chandler. We'd like to ask you a few questions.'

'By what right?' Donna demanded. And we were off. I yawned. I've been in these scenarios before. Veiled malice from the peelers, alarmed indignation back, then they let you go saying you're cleared but with hatred in their hearts. At least, that's the script. I wondered if there was any such thing as an antique police truncheon lying around. The building seemed old enough, and coppers' items are very desirable collectibles nowadays. I perked up wondering how to work the conversation round to antiques. The costliest old truncheons have a police district lettered in black and gold. Then I put my foot in it.

'Your car was reported stolen,' Chandler said.

'By me,' Donna said. 'A misunderstanding.'

God, I thought. The silly woman bubbled me when I'd shot Nottinghamwards. 'I found it abandoned,' I improvised with a grovel. 'And brought it back.'

'And you are . . .?'

'Lovejoy.' As I spoke Donna suddenly made a half-turn. Her hand moved. I could have sworn she'd all but asked me to shut up. The policewoman giggled at my name. The uniformed bobby laughed resonantly. 'I'm only an antique dealer, in this lady's employ.'

'Employ? For how long, Lovejoy?' He gave the bent eye to the policewoman. She scurried out.

'Couple of days.'

I glanced at Donna, hoping she wouldn't mention Tinker. The boozy old sod was out there somewhere, plodding in our wake. Donna's face was white and drawn. What the hell was going on? Maybe she'd suddenly received bad news from Cardew.

Chandler made us write our details, age and address. I'm not joking when I say I was scared. Cop shops always put the wind up me so I was relieved when Chandler was called out to the phone. The bobby pointedly sat watching, clearing his throat whenever we moved.

'That's our taxes you've wasted on the blower,' I said

when Chandler returned. He pointed at me and sat. His face had that knowing look the Old Bill always put on when they've sussed out your record. He must have contacted Ledger, my home-town peeler.

'Right. Mrs Vernon. What are you doing in this man's company? He's a villain.'

'I hired him,' she answered. She was becoming as unreliable as me, and I didn't like it. 'Casual rates. He was highly recommended by a friend in Nazewell.'

'Purpose?' The policewoman was working a tape-cassette. Why they don't learn to write I'll never know.

'To advise on antiques.' She paused. 'He hasn't been very successful so far, unfortunately.'

'Your husband's name, please?'

'Sidney Charles Vernon. Antique dealer. He isn't at home just now.'

Here it came. I was looking at Donna, fascinated. I'd learned more important negatives in the last few seconds than I had since that seance. Even cop shops have their uses.

'Mrs Vernon. Do you know anyone by the name of Chatto? Ken Chatto?'

'No. Should I?' She had tautened, yet her voice remained full of calm. It was the dive off the springboard, the throw of the dice. More and bigger lies were on the way. 'Why do you ask?'

'Your husband was reported in his company a week ago. In this area.'

'My husband's in Somerset,' Donna said. 'Your report is wrong. He said something about Cornwall.'

'His car registration, then?'

'He probably left by train . . .'

It was all great stuff. I listened admiringly, fable after fable trotting out. Or, I thought anxiously, was what she'd told me the genuine lies while Chandler was only getting the fake lies? Or was my version the truly false lie, as a bluff?

I got a headache and switched off. There was a print of one of Modigliani's longish faces hanging behind the police desk. Amazing where culture gets to. I found myself smiling, because Elmyr de Hory forged that very painting, and his fakes go for the price of a house nowadays. De Hory is the greatest of all fakers of modern masters, even if he was Hungarian. I don't hold that against him. People say that gallery in Santa Fe's all but cornered the market . . .

'What're you grinning at, Lovejoy?'

I came to. Chandler was glaring. 'Er, sorry. Nice picture,' I said humbly.

He let us go then, but clearly still thought we were up to all sorts. 'Let me know your whereabouts, once daily.'

We left down a long tiled corridor, steps down between brick banisters, a blue lamp with one bulb gone, a bobby leaning his bike against the kerb. A small street, a few cars and a library over the road. Donna said nothing, drove us out of the main street heading east.

'Lucky old us,' I said brightly.

Still nothing. This, I thought with bitterness, is the woman who'd ballocked me for seeing that a beautiful Russian antique received justice and two infants got their dinner. Life's unfair to me and it's usually women that see to it.

'Wonder if we'll catch Sid up before we get to Somerset,' I speculated. Instead we were heading for Lowestoft, the opposite way.

Still nothing? A police car in a lay-by watched us go by. I turned, adjusted the wing mirror. Sure enough its headlights flashed once. Broad daylight. An average blue saloon pulled out at the nearby crossroads and settled in our wake.

'How is Chatto these days, Donna?'

'I'll tell you later, Lovejoy.'

Terse, but definite progress. An hour ago she'd have castrated me for using her first name. Now we were in deep there were only two choices: I'd get the sailor's elbow and be nudge-splashed at the next roundabout, or she'd keep me on because now something had gone seriously wrong with Hubby Sid's scam—and the clue lay in that oddly phoney police interview.

'Hey,' I cackled suddenly, remembering a bagged pasty and some russell rolls I had in my pocket, and hauled them out.

'Have one?' I offered her a roll. 'Er, there's only one pasty, I'm afraid. Sorry.'

She shook her head, driving steadily, but gave a half laugh. 'Lovejoy, I think you're slightly insane. Are you always odd?'

'Do without, then.' The nerve of the bloody woman. Sod her. I'd have the lot. Anyway, it's not me that's odd. It's everybody else. Including Chandler.

She gave that incredulous near-laugh again. We made the next roundabout and she didn't sling me out. Odder still.

The unmarked police car drifted off our tail in Old Nelson Street, Lowestoft. We were left unhindered and found a quiet little tavern pretending it was a hotel. Politely we arranged to meet for supper. I promised on my honour not to make any move without asking her first. It was getting on towards evening.

Then I slipped out and spent a fortune phoning around as darkness fell and the harbour lights lit up from South Basin to Hamilton Dock. I couldn't raise Margaret but Lydia was in and the phone mercifully reconnected. Between assurances (no, I wasn't cold; yes, I was putting my dirty clothes in the plastic bags provided for the purpose; no, I wasn't being rude to Mrs Vernon; yes, she was keeping her distance) I got her to search the names of antique dealers. Chatto, K. W. Esq. lived in Nazewell at a shop called Chatto and Vernon. Aha. I told Lydia my address in case Tinker rang, and said to suss this Chatto bloke out.

'Somebody must know him,' I said.

'Very well, Lovejoy. Oh, could you please get in touch with Madame Blavatsky? Urgently. It must be important, Lovejoy.'

'I promise,' I said, to shut her up, then went into my act. 'The police pulled me in for interrogation.'

'That's utterly scandalous!' she bleated. 'I shall protest immediately!'

'Please don't,' I cautioned anxiously, but I was delighted because she would, too. Detective-Sergeant Ledger would have to tell her why Chandler had been asking after Chatto and Vernon. My way of finding out.

'No, Lovejoy,' she said sternly. 'It's a citizen's responsibility . . .' I could imagine her mouth trying to set grimly, showing how empires were won.

'My coins are gone,' I interrupted. The call was costing a fortune, but indulging women's prejudices always does. I've found that. 'Look. Suss out Sidney Charles Vernon too.'

'Lovejoy!' Lydia exclaimed, scandalized. 'You aren't suggesting—?'

'Something underhand? Now, *would* I?' I left smiling. And committed a terrible, terrible crime.

I forgot Owd Maggie's message.

'Were those beads really worth all that money?' So much for Donna the dedicated antique dealer. 'Those beads' indeed.

'You'd no right to look at that cheque,' I said. We were slightly befuddled from the wine. Only four other tables were occupied, and the people were not bothered with us. It was an ancient nook-and-cranny place, the sort where lovers go to commemorate anniversaries or start new ones. I needn't add that we'd chosen it by accident.

'You could have kept it. It was made out to you.'

Michaela had given me ten per cent in notes. 'I'd got my commission.'

The nosh place was a little dump near The Scores, a tangle of cobbled streets in the old town. I was feeling oddly contented. Donna was defrosting. And we were near my own territory, out on the coastal estuaries where I get to hear of most things by osmosis.

Neither of us mentioned Sid nor the mysterious Ken Chatto whose name uttered by Sergeant Chandler had sent her pale. Loosened, she talked of this dream she had, of becoming such a good sociologist that she would iron out all the world's problems. I was polite and didn't yawn. I'm kind deep down.

Then I got reminiscing, nearly my only fault. The antique fakes, the old fiddle trick pulled with oil paintings. I told her about the boom in antique musical instruments (and who created it). And, laughing, of a hitherto unknown pre-Raphaelite painting (and who created that). And how frantic the East German currency dealers are, now they've learned about Italian middlemen. She was intrigued, her eyes shining. And of a fake called Equal Freedom I'd given to the hospice exhibition. 'Filled with Polyfilla and old nails and said it was bronze, nothing fancy.'

She was quizzically amused. 'Rob the rich to give to the hospice? It has a familiar ring, Lovejoy.'

I was indignant. 'People who buy art for investment are the worst sort of criminal. They steal our antiques, then hold them to ransom.'

'You're a romantic. Can't you see that antiques are all simply money?'

'Can't you see they are all simply not?'

She did her sad fifty per cent laugh again. I had to explain, but why do I bother? Women are rotten listeners. They only hear what they agree with.

'Tell me, Donna. What do you think you're doing? Not,' I continued over protest, 'chasing Sidney or whatever. But this very minute.' She was puzzled. 'Feeding your face? Wondering how much that bird at the corner table paid for her frock? Well, there was no such lax moment for the man who made that chair in 1755.' In the corner stood a lovely old chair with a red cord to stop anybody sitting on it, Chippendale period. 'That chairmaker had no chance of living to old age. Half his children died before they were one year old. He slogged a hundred hours a week for a pittance in a slum that'd turn our hair, and slept on woodshavings. He could be sacked at whim, and would then starve. He owned nothing except his pants, shirt and clogs if he were lucky.'

'So? Times change.'

'But his chair hasn't, love.' I was so narked by her response I rose, hauled her up and yanked her over to the corner. The other couples watched us in silence. 'Look at the back legs. They curve *in every plane*! How thick did the wood have to be? Come on. Answer.'

'Two feet? Four feet?'

'Seven inches, love. A miracle, because he *felt* the living wood as he went, stroke by stroke. He'd never tasted wine, tea, coffee or sugar in his life, never seen an orange, couldn't afford any book, never worn a hat, never touched soap or drunk clean water.' I was so mad I nearly clocked her. 'You see, Donna? Whoever he was, he loved his work even in hell. His chair's telling you all this. And I'm proud of him.'

Donna looked across at the beautiful piece. What a sight a complete set must have been.

'Touch it and you touch him, back across the centuries. See? Antiques are how we hit back at Time.'

'I'll believe you,' she said. It was to shut me up.

Her hand covered mine a moment. She was in midnight blue, with a simple vee neck and a Victorian pearl necklace. I was worried about her larger pearls. One or two were looking a bit barrelled from wear, but they were a good try. I love pearls. Her nails were long and gleaming, her hands and skin good. Maybe this Ken Chatto bloke was her . . .

Well. My face must have given the thought away because her hand moved. She rose to pay our bill, saying, 'We don't want Lydia turning up to argue the contract, do we?' From Donna Vernon that was a joke.

We went for a walk towards the coastguard station for half an hour. She linked arms with me. We didn't say much more.

At the tavern she took her key and went straight up because we wanted to make an early start. I decided on a nightcap in the taproom.

While I was chatting the barmaid up Lydia rang. She'd been trying to reach me all evening. Maggie Hollohan had had an accident. She'd passed away shortly after help had arrived.

Sometimes it takes a shock to make you realize you've just been buggering about doing nothing. I snatched three cheese rolls and a bottle of Bulmer's from the taproom, and moved. Three minutes flat and I was zooming out of Lowestoft on the A12, driving like the clappers.

CHAPTER 9

The car needed filling with petrol within a few desperate miles, which only goes to show how thoughtless Donna was. Not that she'd known that I was going to nick her motor, but she might at least have filled the damned thing. I was at the mortuary after a fast scarey drive along East Anglia's winding night roads.

A bobby called Jock Ellis recognized me from past encounters with the peelers, but he knew precious little. Nothing new for the Old Bill.

'She was down an alley down the Dutch Quarter,' Jock said. 'A couple found her. She'd been duffed up.'

'St Martin's Lane? Actors?' It was a guess. The amateur

dramatics people always go home through there after rehearsal.

'Who told you? Here, Lovejoy. Never knew Owd Maggie was a friend of yours.'

One of those terrible moments came when every word seems horrendous. Friend. Yours. Was. Jock got the technician to show me Owd Maggie's mortal remains. I welled up. The poor old dear had plasters on her veins where the ambulance people had infused them. She'd been battered, caked blood and dirt everywhere on her sparse hair. Her spectacles were in a manilla envelope on the tray beneath. Her feet had come uncovered. I pulled the sheet over her toes and tucked them in. Don't you do some daft things. St Martin's Lane is an ancient narrow little alley in the part we call the Dutch Quarter, after Flemish weavers settled there yonks ago. Picturesque, with alleys and lanterns and quietude.

'Couldn't you at least have washed her hands?' I heard myself ask in a thick voice. Murder—indeed any death—contradicts all norms.

'Ledger said not to, Lovejoy.' The man was apologetic. 'Coroner's case, see.'

Police, the law, and medicine therefore scored my question stupid. Well, if they scored me I'd score them. High time that Lovejoy began to use his cerebral cortex, always assuming. Our town's as peaceable as they come—this murder might even drive fowlpest off the *County Standard*'s headlines—but the Dutch Quarter leads nowhere. It's a nook between the Castle, our ruined priory, and a hedged park.

'Why the Dutch Quarter?' I asked.

'Yes, why, Lovejoy?' And there stood Ledger, really great.

'Sly old Jock,' I reproved. 'You phoned in, eh?'

'Well done, Constable,' Ledger said. Jock looked proud but shy. You'd think they'd caught Jack the Ripper. And our safety's in the hands of nerks like these.

'Stop congratulating each other,' I said nastily. 'Explain why you got Owd Maggie killed.'

Ledger's a mundane-looking bloke, as these go. He has a doggy moustache, hornrims, a waistcoat and watch-chain, and uses after-dinner speakers' tricks—patting pockets, aheming—to slow up conversations and give his lonesome neurones time to synapse. I have a theory that he's really a publicity-still from the 1950s.

'Lovejoy,' Ledger was saying, *ex cathedra*. 'You're coming down to the station to make a statement as to the extent of your involvement.'

I stared, incredulous. 'As to the extent of my involvement? It must be these bloody courses they keep sending you peelers on. You all come back talking like the Home Secretary. You ignorant burke. I wouldn't go to church with you, let alone your neffie clink.'

He was tough, but law-bound. The mortuary technician was looking in, wanting to close up. Jock had finished his report. He'd made two carbon copies in his alphabet-soup scrawl. I wanted one. Distraction was called for.

'Did you know that Confucius was a police inspector, Ledger?' I walked across, giving the morose technician a shove into Jock. 'And Gandhi was a stretcher-bearer like you, burke. Standards are falling.'

'Here, nark it.' The technician and Jock were in a heap.

'Right, Lovejoy,' Ledger was saying, but I'd scrambled across them and out of the door. Nobody chased me. I made the hospital car park unhindered and drove sedately out along the road to our village. It's not far. I made it just as the night's pitch was weakening. Old Kate's cottage light was on. Today she would take her joint to be cooked in our village baker's oven, after the first bread batch was drawn at four o'clock. They still do this in country villages, get the baker's oven to do roasts and dry the bedsheets on rainy washdays.

A quick brew up, and I read Owd Maggie's BID DOA

police report which Constable Ellis had typed. It had been
no bother to nick a carbon copy while the technician and
he tumbled. Brought In Dead—Dead On Arrival. Nothing
I didn't already know. But by the phone in Lydia's writing
were notes I needed.

> Lovejoy,
>   Chatto and Vernon run Spendlate Antiques, Nazewell,
> specializing in antique jewellery, mainly pearls. Remem-
> ber the Siren rumour. They dried about ten weeks ago;
> some deals are in abeyance. Take care.
>
> Lydia.

About midnight I set off to Lowestoft deep in thought.
My mind went: Donna Vernon's husband Sid embarks on
an antique sweep. Off he goes, and is now long overdue.
Donna collars me; off we chase. Fortunately we have a list
of where he's supposed to have gone. Partner Chatto seems
to have joined him, and this upsets Donna. And she'd
pretended ignorance of Chatto. For my benefit, or Chandler's? And why? Chatto is Sid Vernon's partner in Spendlate
Antiques. Chandler pulls me and Donna to suss out what
relationships exist between the four of us, if any. I had
this odd feeling that everything—Chandler's interview as
well—was part of a play.

Flaw One: if Sid's trying to escape Donna, why is he
leaving such a well-marked track? Flaw Two: Sid is even
thicker than your average antique dealer, the world's greatest known epsilon-minus nerks. His performance so far
had been pathetic: not caring about a genuine aigrette, not
spotting Reverend Cunliffe's pricey box of genuine cards,
dismissing Ellen Smith's brilliant gedanite rosary when he
could have wheedled it off her for a song. Flaw Three:
Owd Maggie is killed. Maybe somebody had overheard me
phoning Lydia in the Lowestoft pub last night, and actually
believed Owd Maggie had received some urgent spiritual

telecast? I certainly didn't number Donna among the believers, so she was clear. Funny how that pale thin geezer kept coming to mind. Maybe he'd overheard in the taproom, hurtled south and . . . I shivered.

Following my headlights northwards on the A12, I thought of Spendlate Antiques. To everybody else they'd look a decent little wandering syndicate of buyers who exported to the Continent, cash on the nail for good stuff.

But from now on they spelled pearls.

You've got to hand it to oysters and other molluscs. When you think of it, they live a pretty grotty life stuck in the mud until somebody slices through their valve muscle and eats them alive (sorry about this gruesome bit). Not only that, but the whole world hopes they're diseased, by a speck of a parasite or sand working under the shell or into the mollusc's body. Why? Because the desperate little creature tries to cure itself by secreting conchiolin and calcium carbonate as tiny prisms of calcite or aragonite. This nacre forms in thin onionskin layers and looks shiny. The entire blob of disease is a pearl. And the poor mollusc never complains. Not that it's got much to complain with, just a lot to complain about. Seems to me that animal rights societies should care for the downtrodden mollusc, if only they'd bother.

Lydia's list of Spendlate's activities included a lot of Victorian jewellery. Pretty low value, nothing tremendous, yet always there in local auction records. Lydia'd done a good job.

A year ago somebody put word around of a genuine variant of the Canning Siren for sale. The Siren's what we call a 'oncer': there's nothing else like it, though crude late Prussian and German derivatives abound. She's about 1585, Italian. I've never seen her though I know plenty who were at Sotheby's when she was sold for a fortune. It's a pendant made of gold, jewels and enamel, arranged in the form of a siren, a lovely lady who hangs about rivers and oceans and sings you to your doom. This siren holds a diamond mirror and is doing her hair with a golden comb. Of course the workmanship is dazzling, and of course it's practically priceless. The point is that the Siren is a single baroque pearl. Baroque means rather bizarre in shape, 'wrong' when compared with the spherical pearl that most people think the 'right' shape. This one happens to be shaped like a woman's torso, breasts and all. The pendant's provenance is impressive, from the time she was given by a Medici duke to a Moghul emperor in 1648 right down to when Lord Canning bought it as First Viceroy of India after the King of Oudh got up to no good. You can guess what a splash the story of a Canning Siren variant created among us dealers. A variant's a genuine similar piece, made in the same materials by the same hands—and costing more or less the same. Think of another *Last Supper* by da Vinci, and you have it.

This rumour, like all really interesting ones, died the death. It was always a long shot. The craftsmanship needed to adapt these baroque shapes into centaurs, dragons and butterflies died out with the Renaissance jewellers of Italy and Spain. But for a few days, while that luscious rumour circulated, every antique dealer in East Anglia licked his chops and prayed that the Siren variant would come his way. Common sense sadly prevailed and we all sobbed into our ale, because huge high-quality baroque pearls just simply aren't found in these days of standardized conformity in the pearl farms of Japan and the Arabian Gulf. Too good to be true, in other words.

Now, the one name that kept cropping up when the Siren rumour was doing the rounds was Spendlate Antiques.

By driving like the clappers I was in the tavern in Lowestoft in fair time. I had a three millisec bath, and was languidly noshing breakfast when Donna Vernon came down. She looked radiant, dazzling the few occupants of the breakfast-room with her smile, glowing with health and beauty, dressed to kill.

'You look a rag, Lovejoy.'

'What else is new?' I offered her toast to be going on with. If she wasn't an enemy I'd fall for her. 'Actually, I thought all night of a certain person.'

She pinked and shoved at her hair like they do. 'None of that, Lovejoy. We have too much to do today.'

'Exactly.' Oh cunning, cunning Lovejoy. 'We've dallied and dillied too long. I'll show you how a real antique sweep is done. Eat,' I commanded, trying to sound like a granny, 'and save the world trouble.' My mind felt free-falling and white-hot. The grub nearly choked me but I was behaving beautifully. Until now I'd meekly done as I'd been told. Hereon it'd be speed and light. Owd Maggie'd died because I'd dawdled. 'I'll find Sid for you, love.'

As God's my judge I'll find him, I thought with grim piety.

She eyed me with a doubtful smile.

'Nice pearls you had on last night,' I added as the fried eggs arrived. 'Time they were re-strung. I noticed the nacre was going at their equator . . .'

CHAPTER 10

My tiredness evaporated. I was actually grinning as Donna drove us out on the A146 towards Beccles, me urging speed and going demented when I mislaid her list. I'd got the antiques fever on me, that berserk craving that makes you certain of antique everything. Immediately. Yesterday an indolent drifter doubting your own name, today you bullet about in a mental ferment. You pull antiques by magnetism. I swear that luscious antique items catch the feeling too, and think: Thank God a proper divvie's arrived and will instantly spot that I'm a genuine 1790 Boule inkstand, and will stop me being used as a frigging button-jar in this neffie cupboard. And they leap into your arms with a squeak of joy. Don't laugh. I really believe that antiques feel this way. If you disagree, you don't deserve any and it's your own fault.

Not only that, but other dealers recognize it. And they bow to your unstoppable passion. It is utterly exhilarating. They fetch out of hiding their specials, their sleepers, their savers which they've been gloating over for years. Safes are opened. Dusty drawers unlocked. Truth, believe it or not, is told whereas normally antique dealers infarct at the first glimpse of sincerity. Divvying out-magics them all.

'Only three miles before we reach Barnby, Donna. Can't you go any faster?'

She gave that exasperated deposit of a laugh. 'What is the matter with you today, Lovejoy? I want no chauvinist sexist moves from you,' she said. It was meant as a slight mockery of her old style.

'You'll get none, love,' I said. 'And that's the truth.' I beamed sickeningly into her puzzlement. I got her to park off the intersection while I walked down the unmade road.

The Barnby address was a newish semi-detached house, three bedrooms, k.&b., garage and garden, lvg rm, dng rm, and a wife with a flowery apron holding a paint brush heavenwards. Seagull emulsion, not a bad colour for a hallway. She looked fourteen, bless her heart, in enormous yellow household gloves. She was badly in need of another arm to keep her hair out of her eyes.

'Mrs Sutton? I'm Mr Vernon's partner,' I said. Not that much of a lie. 'I came about the antique. You advertised, I believe?'

'Yes. Mr Vernon changed his mind, then?'

'Not really. I'm the expert, love. Here.' I extracted her hairclip and clumsily shoved it back with her locks trapped in it. 'Your hair's in a worse state than China.'

'I know,' she said, embarrassed but smiling. 'This decorating. I've so much to do. Mind. Everything's wet paint.'

'Does Mr Sutton mind you selling, erm . . .?'

Into her face came that toxic scorn wives show. As if they realize that any man gullible enough to promise to clothe, feed and provide for a woman for life deserves all he gets. It's an expression you often see in cosy company before blood flows.

She showed me the rectangular glass plaque standing on a table, held in an ebony stand. 'The engraving's supposed to have been done by somebody quite good,' she said a little nervously. 'The glass is old, though.'

Aye, I thought sadly, but not as old as me. The faker's idea was good, because glass slabs were made even in Roman days for decoration. You get all sorts of engraved ones, mosaics, enamelled ones even, opaque whitish plaques, painted scenes. Some look really very effective with scenic pictures on them. Early Egyptian and Roman, and 17th-century Bohemian, plaques are worth a fortune. This thing was dross, a pathetic new thing, ostentatiously dated 1804, showing some country house or other. I touched it to make sure, and not a vibe, not a single mental chime of authenticity. And, do you know, that glorious power was so absolute that I smiled, not disappointed in the least. Because I *felt* something here in the house. I was warm all over. Something was excitely pealing *I'm here, I'm here.* Sounds daft, I know, but I went mesmerized into the lvg rm and laughed aloud to see it there on the wall.

'Hello, sweetheart,' I said to the painting. 'My name's Lovejoy.'

It hung there all bashful, a small landscape painting. Most painters have a hundred per cent individual style. See one, and you can spot Richard Wilson's work for life. Thirty years ago you could get a genuine painting for a fiver. God's truth. Richard Wilson painted with his own unmistakable hand no fewer than twenty-five variants of his landscape *The White Monk*. Even London dealers have let Wilsons go for peanuts because their textbooks tell them that the 'original' is in some posh gallery. And remember that the great Turner himself started as a humble apprentice copy-painter, so that non-Girtin Girtin copy your auntie's got might in fact have been painted by a greater genius still. I felt a right twerp when Mrs Sutton brought me back to earth.

'You're talking to the painting!' she exclaimed.

'Ah.' I came to. 'Er, a print like it hung on my nursery wall when I was little. Nice to see it again.'

I turned as if to go. She said, 'Do you like it?'

In her voice was the housewife's concern for balanced budgetry.

'Well . . .' I said reluctantly. 'You mean your plaque and the painting together? I might be able to stretch a point . . .' The world's fate hung.

'Have you time for a cup of tea?' she said.

Mrs Sutton looked instantly familiar, like one of those actresses who, wives of film producers, suffer relentless over-exposure in afternoon features and telly adverts which doom them to a life brimful of unrealized potential. She deserved better. I liked her.

'Well, I shouldn't . . .'

Donna was fuming when finally I streaked—well, walked —up.

'Do you call that speed, Lovejoy?'

'Hasten, James. And don't spare the horses.' I was desper-ately thinking: Where's Tinker now I need the old sod? I was mad with myself. I should have asked Mrs Sutton if Vernon had asked about pearls.

We made Bungay by eleven o'clock.

Days like that stick in your mind.

We tore among the villages and townships of the Broads. All day a dilute sun reflected from the long waters of East Anglia's inland stretches. Distant sails glided along the dykes and low ridges, triangles of browns, reds, blues and white showing where the boats cut through waterways. More bridges than Venice and glimpses of white motorboats with girls atop front decks. Striped awnings from Mediterranean sunbeaches showing among reeds. Lads splashing near a remote village's wharf, and those little black ducks chugging jerkily across gleaming surfaces. These townships at holiday times seem full of brown limbs and weird yachting caps.

But within minutes of our next address I'd got the pattern, and found yet another flaw.

It turned out to be a houseboat moored at a patch of sudden tidiness in a small river camouflaging itself skilfully along a line of willows and tall reedy stuff. That's the trouble with East Anglia. You think these tangled strips are hedgerows till you splash.

The inhabitant was a young painter, bearded and biblical. When we arrived he was hard at it on the foredeck painting an orange triangle on an octagonal canvas. A cardboard cut-out bird was tacked to the railing. I helloed and paused respectfully on the bank, the way one waits when a magistrate goes to the loo. The houseboat looked on its last legs to me. I wasn't going on that thing at any price and whispered that to Donna when she impatiently ordered me to board. Its chimney had fallen and was stuck-rusted on to the cabin's railing. The mooring ropes had rotted, but the houseboat had remained in place. The bloody wreck couldn't even drift. The painter kept on painting.

'Money,' I called out.

Magic. He dropped his brush. 'Why didn't you say?' With one bound he vaulted free of his artistic chains to the bank beside us. I'd never seen such a tall relic before, living. He was clothed in a series of patches which were vague neighbours rather than closely sewn. 'What kind do you want?'

'Didn't you advertise, erm . . . ?' I said cleverly.

'Oh, in that free paper. Yes.' He wasn't downcast, just hopeful in a newer direction. 'It's over here.' There was a rickety shed nearby, looking stitched up the middle like a Welsh blanket. Ivy and brambles covered it. Butterflies hung about. Birds twittered. God, it was rural. He pulled a rickety door aside. My chest didn't chime, but my heart jumped. Under a mass of rotting planks and sacks stood a bicycle. It took half a second to lift aside enough debris to reveal all.

A Sanaquizzi bicycle is really rather special—metal wheels with forks of strengthened bamboo, believe it or not. They were Continental, made over four slender years from about 1908. Hardly antique, but odd and highly sought. Laugh if you like, but old butcher's-boy bikes, post-office bicycles, lovers' tricycles for spooning while you pedalled like mad and she struggled to keep her elegant bonnet on, represent the greatest of all modern booms. It took everybody by surprise in the 1960s. These 'new antiques', as people call collectibles from 1950 back to 1914, range from a year's average salary to a week's. Please ignore their condition; start bargaining. And, if they're chucking in a suit of grandad's 'bicycling apparel' from the wardrobe, sell your wife to raise the ante.

'A man called. Only talked from the bank. Didn't even take a look. Interrupted my painting of a bittern.'

'Tut-tut,' I sympathized, and looked at Donna. She'd already turned on her heel.

'Sorry, mate. I'm not interested.' I slipped him a scribbled IOU for twenty quid with a wink.

He was quick on the uptake. He glanced after Donna with a veteran's experience of women who criticized his spending the grub money on rose madder and Prussian blue. I looped my finger to show we'd settle up later.

No pearls here either. Pattern: good old Sid was moving faster. Was he sticking to the order of places as listed?

We found the answer in the next two, one in Diss and one

in Eye. Lots of jokes about both names, of course, but not
from me. Both were misses. I didn't care, because they
confirmed my new flaw: Sid Vernon might have nicked
Donna's money and be associating with an evil partner
called Chatto, but he clearly didn't give a damn about
antiques. He was a front, but for whom?

As hunters we too were being pretty lackadaisical, no?
Yes. Because when I'd hurried Donna early this morning
she'd been almost tardy.

The Diss man was a cheerful bloke talking to his three
beehives. He was in his garden smoking a pipe, sitting on a
huge inverted earthenware plantpot. Donna hung back,
thinking him barmy.

He waved me in, quite unabashed. I'd seen it all before.
I whispered to Donna that beekeepers aren't insane, or even
sane come to that. They're just beekeepers. Bad luck if you
don't keep your bees up with the gossip. When he got round
to me it transpired we'd missed Vernon by two days.

'He didn't think much of my antique, I'm afraid,' he said
amiably. 'A local dealer bought it, Jim Prawer. Always
thought it was worth a bit. Little five-legged ivory chair
only a few inches high. Toy, I suppose. Been in my family
years.'

'Christ.' I almost wept. It sounded a genuine antique.
They made the best in Goa for the Portuguese. I thanked
him, said cheerio to his hives.

'They only came about that ivory antique,' he started
telling the bees pleasantly as we left. Well, whatever turns
you on. Still no pearls.

Eye's an ancient old place, the sort you should linger in.
Though it pained me, I urged Donna on through. She was
becoming a bit ratty by then. I was hearty as a breakfast
broadcaster because my very own flawless plan was forming.
I'd had enough of other people's.

The chap was a burly aggressive chap, beery of odour
and piggy of eye. I knocked and asked him politely if his

antique was still for sale. He threatened me by raising his voice and telling me to sod off. The object had been sold to a reliable dealer in Eye.

He re-emerged at a second knock and loomed larger. His beer-belly shoved me off the porch. 'I'll not tell you again,' he bawled.

Blokes like him tire me quickly, like a joke on a seaside cup. 'Look, sir,' I tried pleasantly. 'Your fake antique might be worth a—'

He went deranged. 'Fake?' he howled, forcing me down the garden path by sheer advancing mass. '*Fake?* It was a genuine *America*'s replica. A London silversmith, too, date stamp and everything, 1851. I told that other idiot that I didn't deal with gipsies, so clear off or I'll have the police on you . . .'

I explained to Donna as we rode between hedges to Saxmundham, 'Sid must have been "that other idiot". Getting close, eh?'

'My husband's a warm human being,' she reprimanded frostily.

More socialspeak. As if everybody should have a knighthood for breathing. I settled back, having learned all I wanted from the boatmending baddie: he had said '*America*'s', so he was a true yachtsman who knew 1851 was the date of the first *America*'s Cup Race, exactly right date for a fashionable replica. To me the man was exactly in pattern: a non-antique non-dealer, who'd advertised an antique from a home address.

She drove on in silence, more worried than ever I'd seen her, me smiling and nodding encouragement. We were catching up with the bastard.

None of this was my fault to start with, so what followed when I caught him wouldn't be my fault either, right?

At a tavern in Saxmundham we separated for a few minutes before having a late nosh. I couldn't get Lydia on the blower and I knew Helen was having a big thing with a moneyed civil servant so she'd not be up yet—Helen in love wakes late and smokes her first packet of fags to dog-ends before brewing up. Luckily Margaret was at the White Hart. She was all ready for a long chat but I cut that short and made her take down the details, the Russian gadenite rosary at Michaela French's in Lincoln, the genuine Wilson landscape I'd reserved and its neffie companion the glass plaque at Mrs Sutton's, the genuine Sanaquizzi bike, the miniature ivory chair at dealer Jim Prawer's shop near Diss, and that *America*'s Cup replica now in 'some reliable dealer's hands' in fine reliable Eye.

'I've reserved some, Margaret,' I told her. 'Mrs Sutton's stuff, the bike. The others will have to be bargained for. Get me somebody to do a fixed sweep on a split.'

She went doubtful. 'That'll be difficult.'

'For God's sake, Margaret, I'm on a divvy streak,' I yelled frantically. 'It's money for jam. You?'

'I'm stuck, Lovejoy. I'll search about. Lydia's gone to see Beatrice over something.'

'Drink up and get looking,' I said. I didn't want Lydia. 'I'll ring you at the Arcade in an hour.'

At the right time I gave Donna the slip and got the news from Margaret: she'd got Sandy and Mel for basic expenses and twenty per cent of the gross. I went berserk but she said there was nobody else. They'd already left for Lincoln. She rang off in tears, me blazing. Now I was in even more of a hurry.

My stealthy search round East Anglia was becoming like Trooping the Colour. First Vernon, followed by Chatto, then the police, me and Donna, then Tinker, all now followed—last and noisiest—by Sandy and Mel in the universe's least secret sequin-toting motor-car. Jesus, but I had a headache. At first it was only terrible, but got much worse two seconds later.

CHAPTER 11

Information, like statistics, is rubbish, yet I'm a mine of the stuff. I have an irritating knack with pointless facts. Napoleon perfumed his horse. One acre supports forty-seven thousand tons of air. Richard the Lion-Heart could play every known musical instrument. Turner the painter drank a bottle of sherry a day. I can go on and on.

Connecting facts is different. I'm naturally hopeless.

So at the time I didn't see much significance when police met me in the car park, asked me if I was Lovejoy and drove me about twenty miles to one of their many clinks. Donna, loyal as women always are, pretended she wasn't with me and watched my abduction in silence. I could have been kidnapped for the Turkish galleys or anything. That's women. I kept telling the Old Bill I was heading in the opposite direction and could they please put me down at the next bus stop . . .

Twin constables looking pre-pubertals took me to the cells. These places always have sickly niffs of disinfectant and night soil battling for supremacy. Keys clanked and bars clanged. I was just getting nervous when the leading Old Bill said to me, 'He's in here, sir.' Me. Sir?

'Who is?'

'Wotcher, Lovejoy. Sorry. I wuz nicked.' Tinker was sitting on the cell bunk, grinning apologetically.

'You old sod,' I exploded. 'Where the hell have you been?'

'Drunken vagrant,' the constable said. 'Lucky Sergeant Chandler remembered you, Lovejoy, or this old bugger'd be up before the beak by now.' He unlocked the cell and jerked his head. 'He's let him off in your care.'

Sergeant Chandler actually doing me a favour? I revised my opinion. Until then I'd thought Chandler a right measle, one of those peelers whose mind is frozen into a permanent sneer. Chandler was playing some game.

'Right. Ta. Come on, Tinker.'

Chandler was at his desk when I knocked, the same carefree sprite as always. I heeled the door shut and grovelled my gratitude.

'Think nothing of it, Lovejoy,' he said in his muted foghorn. 'Cheerio.'

I didn't move and said, 'It's cheaper, of course.' He raised his bushy eyebrows. 'To let Tinker go,' I explained.

'Aye?' He sat with fingers interlocked, pious as an oil magnate justifying prices.

God, but peelers are slow these days. No wonder most of them never get promoted out of the billiards room. I helped. 'Isn't this where you show me a photograph of K. Chatto, Esq?'

'Is it, indeed? For what purpose?'

'So at least one of us will know what's going on.'

He didn't smile, just shoved me a photograph. I'd stood all this time, only police being so tired they need chairs. It was that fair-haired weak-faced bloke from Owd Maggie's seance who'd avoided my eyes.

'This is Chatto? What's he done?'

'Only suspicion.' He was trying to sound casual. Little crooks get chased. Big crooks, like Morgan the Pirate, get knighted and freedom. I don't mean bankers and insurance syndicates, incidentally, though if the cap fits . . . 'Seen him before, Lovejoy?'

'No. Should I have done?'

He did smile then. It wasn't pretty. 'Birds of a feather.'

When I reached Saxmundham Donna was furious with me. Not, note, with the police for having snatched me, but me. She came storming up as soon as the police car was out of sight. I felt really narked. I'm the only person in the world who isn't a disadvantaged minority.

'What did they want, Lovejoy?'

'Nothing,' I said sourly. 'They're still on about your car.'

'Are you sure that's all it was?'

I gave her my purest stare. 'Would I lie?'

Oh, I forgot to say I'd got the Old Bill to drop Tinker off just before we'd reached the tavern. I'd scribbled him an instruction, to go on ahead and wait at the last place on our list, near the creek houses in Salcott. Then I'd be shut of the boozy old devil. I was bitter. Cost me a fortune and done nowt.

We started off to do our two addresses near Saxmundham. One was a century-old piece of heavy slag glassware, a blue swirly marble-looking dish by Gateshead's George Davidson—only three slag makers are known for sure, so seeing his lion-and-turret mark was a delight. His company's still around. I got it from a retired policeman, would you believe, again tipping him the wink and dropping a quid and a card so Donna didn't notice. The second was a youngish couple loving in sin on yoghurt and carrots and doing silk-screen printing in somebody's garage. They had a nice finely stitched sampler in a heavy ebony frame showing motifs of birds, flowers and abstract patterns in reds, greens, browns and a blue, which is all usual for 1827. Lovely. A bit unusual to combine eyelet, cross, tent, and some romanian stitches, plus that swinish rococo stitch that always makes you feel a thumb short.

'Unsigned,' I said.

The lank-haired girl shrugged. She was stewing lentils while her skeletal accomplice did appalling designs on a sand tray. 'That's why the man wouldn't buy it.'

Sid Vernon's infallible ignorance was getting on my wick. 'He's a nerk,' I said. Donna gasped. 'It's good. How long ago did he call?'

'Two days.'

On the sly I'd written a few be-prepared cards saying: 'I'll be back and will buy. Deposit enclosed. Lovejoy Antiques, Inc.', each folded with a quid inside. I palmed one to the girl, giving her a look to warn her against Donna. 'We'll think about it. See you. Thanks.'

Exit smiling, resuming journey. Still no pearls.

'We're getting nearer the coast,' I said brightly. 'Do you notice we're travelling almost full circle?'

Now she should have covered that remark, but no. Silence. She'd been quite tough with the mute blame, but I knew she couldn't keep it up. Women are like budgies—don't trust silence. You have to keep revealing your position and intentions, like a destroyer on the move. I can't understand it, because quietness is pretty useful stuff if you want a think. She broke after five miles.

'Is that what you think of my husband, Lovejoy?'

'Well, he's not much of an antique dealer, is he?' I had to say it straight out or she'd become suspicious.

'I suppose your wife was perfect?'

'Pretty good,' I acknowledged to shut her up. The trouble was Cissie always Knew What Was Best, and had morality like other people have bad breath.

That afternoon was gold, pure gold. We found nothing at the house of a retired old violin-maker in Halesworth who'd advertised a boxwood diptych—think of a small folding wooden book shape which opens to reveal dinky scenes of saintly doings. From the old bloke's description it sounded Flemish, genuine, sixteenth century, and I could have strangled the old goon for selling it to a dealer who sounded suspiciously like Big Frank from Suffolk. Still, Big Frank's seventh wife was known to be leading him a dance and he was getting desperate for gelt. Please God Mel and Sandy got their skates on . . .

We followed Vernon's trail to Southwold where musicians bulge the boozers and litter the sands, and I turned my nose up at a baby's feeding-spoon—pap-spoon, they're called— which a pleasant landlady had advertised. Of course I then hurtled back on the pretext of asking if she was related to

the Lancashire Charlestons like me, and slipped her one of
my deposit cards for the precious little silver object. You
can't mistake a pap-spoon, with its hinged lid over the bowl
and hollow handle for, believe it or not, actually blowing
the mashed grub into the obstinate little fiend's mouth.
George would have eaten the spoon.

The delectables went on and on as we roamed the estuary
villages, tumbling on me in a golden rain. It became so
hectic I had to make a pretend dash to the loo in Wickham
Market to scribble another cluster of deposit cards.

Within two hours I'd nailed a so-called 'toothpick' which
was encased in a small whistle. Sounds daft, but Anne
Boleyn even had one designed by Albrecht Dürer. Neither
a manicure instrument nor toothpick, but an ear-scraper.
Its mini-scoop gives its function away. You scrape out your
ear wax with a carefree flourish. It was only base metal and
1760-ish, but unusual enough for me to promise a good price
to the hard-up widow of Leiston whose hens flourished near
the nuclear power station. No pearls.

We missed an old set of English bagpipes, the mellow
sort you work with your arm, but collared a Staffordshire
footbath from a young footballer near Woodbridge. He
actually wanted to sell his 'old pot baking dish' and put
money towards a carburettor. I forgave him because it was
big, almost nineteen inches long, and both its lifting handles
were intact. The vertical sides mean early, say 1805. Anyway, the footballer can't be criticized because I've seen one
used in a fancy house where the charming hostess had also
guessed wrong about what the elegant dish was actually for.
No pearls.

And a Dublin shawl-brooch by West, who, bloody cheek,
registered their Celtic design in 1849, a zillion years after
the original from which they copied was made for some
ancient Celt in County Cavan. The naughty old lady near
Orford Ness who'd advertised it tried telling me it was in
her family for seventeen generations. By now I was prattling

explanations to Donna, but of course boxing clever and still
not letting her know I was putting a deposit down on each.
Vernon had called at them all and blundered on his way.

And from an Ipswich grocer a copy of a red-glazed Ming
stem cup, made locally a century back and lovely. And
an Indo-China Victorian period ultramarine-blue glazed
octagonal dish with bits of the famed black decoration—the
Vietnamese copied the Japanese—that still costs only groats
(give it time, give it time). And from a retired baker near
Woodbridge's ferry . . .

Just before seven we booked in to a Woodbridge inn.
We'd planned to meet for supper at nine o'clock because
Donna was tired. I said I'd have a glass before I went to
rest. Sure enough, she came down a few minutes later to
say she was really too exhausted to turn out. She'd have a
meal brought to her room and did I mind. I said not in the
least; I'd have some pasties in the taproom. We were so
polite. Enemies are character-forming, aren't they? I wasn't
sure who mine were, but if she'd blown the gaff to Sid
Vernon or Chatto about Owd Maggie's urgent message,
well, she was one of the worst I'd got.

The hire car came two minutes after I'd phoned. Gave
me just enough time to telephone my list to Margaret Dainty
and tell her to relay the details to Mel and Sandy, wherever
they might have got to.

'Are you all right, Lovejoy?' Margaret asked. 'You sound
bitter.'

'I'm fine, love.' I told her to contact the *Advertiser* and say
I was coming in. I was collecting allies and foes like a
harvester does grain. Opponents are okay; it's allies that
worry me.

CHAPTER 12

The *Advertiser* offices are three storeys tall, which is big for our town. It's a trick, really. They have only five tiny rooms, a shared loo and broom cupboard. For a few quid a year they're allowed to hang this enormous neon shingle outside.

Practically the whole *Advertiser* is Liza. She wears a green eyeshade, as a joke, and works all hours. She smokes cheroots, wears gunslinger jeans, bishop blouses and a Teddyboy string tie. I like her. Liza smiles at people before being introduced, which in most women's book indicates at least a harlot.

'I'm too frigging busy to have you wasting my bloody time, Lovejoy,' Liza said in welcome. She prides herself on her breasts and teeth, and is developing this akimbo pose to show off these features. Doc Holliday without the tubercular cough.

'I only want a clipping, Lize. Two minutes. I'm in a hurry.' I didn't want Donna detecting my absence.

'I give you shit-stingy locals free fucking adverts. Now you want free everything else.'

I listened patiently. She'd done sociology.

'We've got to read your rubbish, Lize.'

'Liza, Lovejoy. With a frigging zed.' She unglued her pose and riffled through a cupboard. 'Be quick, before the sodding photocopier goes on the frigging blink. Regional or district?'

'Regional. And pretty recent.' The *Advertiser* is sent out free with local papers. I started on them, working backwards. 'How do you make it pay, Lize?'

'Liza, you reactionary pig. Who said it pays?'

'Ah.' I waggled a chiding digit and worked the photocopier. They were all there in the one issue. Some, like Joe

the parson and Mrs E. Smith, had given their full addresses.
Others had only given phone numbers, yet Donna's address
list for the sweep was fuller. And so far we had visited about
half.

'Ta, Lize. See you soon, eh?'

'Liza, you imperialist fascist bastard . . .'

Maybe she and Donna went to the same university. I left
with two copies of the antique adverts column. How can
women be practically the same shapes and turn out so
different? It's a rum old world. So one issue of the old
Advertiser was Vernon's entire source. And no pearls in the
list. I drove to the harbour.

A light was on in Beatrice's bedroom. Barney came to the
door blocking out the light from the stairs. He wore a Fair
Isle pullover and trousers, no shoes. A hasty dresser. I
grinned apologetically.

'Wotcher, Barney. Lydia sent me.' Well, it sounded more
honest.

'Lydia came the other night,' Barney grumbled.

'Yes, but she wants a couple of, er, zodiac things cleared
up.'

'It's a nuisance.' He reluctantly let me pass. I knew how
he felt. Being suddenly prised off Beatrice by an interloper
gets you riled. Anybody'll tell you.

Beatrice was dishevelled but covered up. She was shoving
cushions into a semblance of order. In the light Barney was
even bigger. I made a few hearty comments on sailing
weather. Beatrice was smiling as she prepared drinks, un-
asked, and sat opposite me with an alarming display of leg.
I had to look away to start my voice off.

'Donna Vernon was with a bloke, Beatrice?'

'When Mrs Vernon asked me to fix the seance with
Madame Blavatsky? Yes.'

'Did you see him?' I remembered Beatrice looking down
from her window at me.

Beatrice nodded, giving me a knowing wink to show she remembered it, too. Barney was staring morosely into his glass, thank God. 'A Sagittarius, I shouldn't wonder.'

'Really?' I said politely, trying to look intelligent.

She smiled, emphatically shook her head. 'I can see why you'd think Taurus, though—'

Taurus? I wasn't thinking anything. I had to nip this junk in the bud, so interrupted. 'Bea. Did Owd Maggie keep records of her, er, customers?'

'No need, Lovejoy.' Beatrice glanced into her glass and sighed. Empty again. I rose quickly to fill it and keep the flow of information coming.

'Somebody else kept them for her?'

'Of course. Cardew.'

I gave her the drink, one glug of gin and two of lemonade. Barney glowered suspiciously. Clang. I'd blundered. 'Erm,' I said, 'I hope that's how you like it, Beatrice. I'm not very good at, er, drinks. Did you say Cardew?'

'Yes.' Beatrice was unmoved. 'It's quite logical, Lovejoy. Madame Blavatsky's memory was awful.'

Silly me. Another headache loomed. 'Look, love. You know I'm not into this seance jazz. Just tell me. Can Cardew be reached?' For all I knew it might be like phoning up.

'Oh, that'd be hard.' Her eyes were shining with interest. This was a challenge. 'It has been done, but—'

Well, if you can't beat them. I said carefully, 'The reason is, Owd Maggie had a message for me. She told Lydia to contact me urgently.'

'And you didn't,' Beatrice said gently.

'No,' I barked. Then said again, 'No,' but quieter. If Barney hadn't been there I'd have given Beatrice a bloody good hiding. There was no need for her to go on about it. I felt bad enough.

'Oh, Lovejoy.' Her eyes filled.

'I know, I know. Somebody must have told Owd Maggie

I was back. I have wood carving lessons with old Connally in his studio down the Dutch Quarter.'

Barney's mind moved momentarily off Beatrice. 'How did they know to say the Dutch Quarter?'

'They didn't,' I guessed. 'They just probably said Lovejoy's around, and followed her until it was opportune to . . . to . . . So if there's a chance of getting her message,' I ended weakly. Barney snorted in derision, embarrassing me. I felt a right twerp.

'Why not simply ask Madame Blavatsky herself?' Beatrice suggested.

'Owd Maggie?' I tried working that out, failed. 'But . . .' My words stuck

'It's so much simpler. And,' she added brightly, 'you can say you're sorry, Lovejoy. Think how nice—'

Now I'd got a blinding headache. 'Can I have that drink, please, Bea? And an aspirin?'

Later I left Beatrice's and phoned Lydia from Charley's, the pub next door. This local nickname means any pub called the Black Buoy. Black Buoy because it sounds like Black Boy, meaning the dark-haired escaped Prince Charles, and that the pub's regulars were secret royalists. Later Charles II of Nell Gwynne fame. She told me to ring a number about ten o'clock for Sandy, and that Tinker had at last reached the cottages at Salcott marshes.

'Oh, aye?' I hadn't forgiven him for the police cells episode.

'He wants to know can he please go home?'

My helper. 'He's *got* no home,' I said sourly. He currently lives in a derelict market van near the flour mill. 'He'd only get sloshed. He can get just as drunk on the waterside,' I argued, getting even more narked at the lazy old devil.

Lydia hesitated. Here it came, the seductive wheedle. 'He hates it out there, Lovejoy. He says it's spooky.'

'Where?' I asked. I'd told the old nerk anywhere within

reach of the old creek cottages near Salcott Knights. I know
it sounds like a spot marked X but it's really half a solar
system wide.

Then in the gloom she spoke an old, old name that
suddenly chilled my nape. It haunts me yet. Not on any
map. But I knew instantly it was the trysting-place towards
which we'd been journeying all along. The long-dead
ancient name rose like a hand from black water.

'Pearlhanger,' she said.

Don't get the wrong idea. Just because I burgled Spendlate
Antiques that night it doesn't mean I was falling for Donna
Vernon. No. I really was still determined to bring Owd
Maggie's murderers to justice. I mean, somebody less honest
and fair-minded might have weakened by now, and been
compelled to raid Vernon and Chatto's antique shop to find
proof that they weren't in league with Donna. So because I
wasn't becoming hooked on Donna, I was absolutely certain
I was still acting in the interests of truth and justice. See
the logic?

Night isn't much help to the East Anglian burglar. A
moving car after midnight in these small townships stands
out like a durbar in a desert, and there's always one nosey
dozy Old Bill smoking in some doorway. Wisely I parked
under a hedge a mile outside the first lamp—the whole
village only had a dozen, thank God—and walked in through
a fine drizzle.

Spendlate Antiques Ltd was a tatty place in the High
Street. The shopfront had seen no paint for years. The
shingle was skewiff as if it had been done by a school-leaver
for a quid. There was no sign of life, the village's few streets
empty. A distant car droned into silence on the A-road.
Soporific. An alarm-system box gave me a momentary
thrombosis, but I guessed it was sham like on most places
and paused briefly at the grimy window. One of those orange
street lamps shone about sixty feet off, showing the usual

clutter of the provincial junkshop: a stool, two chairs, scattered cavalry buttons, a brass pot, some Great War bayonets and medals, some indeterminate crockery, a personal 1725ish sealed wine bottle but faked from recycled glass —one mint original will buy you a fortnight's free holiday or a thousand pasties, according to your station in life. This junk trove was protected by a Suffolk latch and a cottager-lock which were twice as valuable as the muck inside.

Feeling that life wasn't helping me much, I did the wise thing once I'd trembled the lock—the easiest thing in the world with anything bent—and shut the door.

'Hello?' I called. 'Anybody there? It's me.'

Nothing.

A house tells you if it's empty, doesn't it? Scientists, that crowd of aggropaths who make a comfortable living out of fears, tell us it's hormonal smells that are the give-away. All balls, of course. It's simply the inanimate speaking to the animate. The walls and rafters and rooms call a gentle welcome, or howl an implacable hatred, as soon as a person walks within. I really believe this. You don't need Owd Maggie's ghostly Cardew to tell you. Your own apartment, bungalow, caravan trailer, will pulse it at you. Some habitations are right for you, others aren't. That's all there is to it.

This dump was friendly, for all its humble status.

Antique dealers always have a nook. If it's a lock-up shop the nook will never be on the premises. If the a.d. lives there, it will be upstairs, and in a wall. Confidently I went up the stairs and put the bedroom light on. Basically a two-up, two-down pad. The nook was behind a small gilt wall-mirror, some nerk's idea of Machiavellian cleverness.

Three letters. All were signed 'Donna'. All talked to Darling, Lover, Ken, Sweetheart. Plus a pet name which I won't disclose because I'm sure they'd want to keep 'Sexman' confidential.

I wasn't depressed. No, honest. I'm being really frank about it, because after all people go through phases. Clearly Donna was a victim of some crush on that insipid curly-headed oaf called Chatto. Now, women always try to be responsible creatures, stick to patterns and all that. But they lack judgement. And everything's judgement, right? These letters in my hand were a transparent example of a lovely woman, too innocent, falling for the pretty-boy patter of that goon Chatto. A wave of sympathy for Donna swept over me. If she hadn't majored in academic thought she'd know more about humanity. A tragic paradigm for us all. She'd been enticed into trusting a nerk when there were reliable unselfish blokes like me about.

No information about pearls, though. They weren't all that careless.

'So-long,' I told the house, nicked a decomposing um-brella from the window display, and hoofed it back to the car.

Everything's people. It's true. Forget this and all is lost. Which proves that removing people is the ultimate crime. That's why I was heartbroken about Owd Maggie. Loony, what with her seances and everything, but still one of us. That contact with all the antiques in the sweep had restored me a bit, given me reassurance about the purpose of exist-ence, but I was still narked. And I was focused on my own area, those tangled woods, rivers, fields and estuaries they call the Eastern Hundreds. It lies beyond the region's only fair-sized town, which as far as I'm concerned is where civilization ends. But the last few places on the list lay out there. Down one of those creeks Tinker waited. And Vernon and Chatto.

To the best of my ability I'd done what Donna wanted, gone with her entire charade from that seance down the trail among the antiques.

From now on I'd do the deciding.

CHAPTER 13

Just before ten I phoned Sandy about the arrangements about Mrs Sutton's painting. He spent twenty demented minutes criticizing her. ('Lovejoy I mean have you ever *seen* such *teeth* before I *mean* and what *hair*. Oh the Government should do something—') More time wasted.

'Have you got the stuff so far?' I asked hopelessly into his chatter. Talking to Sandy's like shouting at a typhoon, all effort and no use.

'Yes, but at what *cost*! Mrs Teeth-and-Hair was *trying* to make a salad we watched her my *God* Mel had one of his giddy spells and you *know* what he's like about mayonnaise a *lunatic*—'

This hysteria was actually an argument for another one per cent. Wearily I agreed. Anything to keep him and Mel on the move. I couldn't face the thought of the sweep going to waste.

'Mel says it's a deal,' Sandy trilled. His voice sank to a conspiratorial whisper. 'He's absolutely *drooling* at the sound of that triangular-bird painter, Lovejoy! He's thinking of having his hair done. Do you think he should? I mean I've been against his autumn-pink rinse *from the very start* . . .'

The journey gave me chance to think. Donna's whole search was a fraud. Vernon had no real idea about antiques. I'd seen it all, good antiques, duff, frauds, neffies, replicas, ringers, rubbish, and some that we should be buying tickets to look at. Vernon hadn't bothered with a single one. Nor had Donna. It only struck me today that if we'd really wanted to find him we should have done it the other way round: started at the last place on the list, Salcott marshes.

Then why did she hire me? And why was she so distressed when Chandler faced her?

It had occurred to me that Owd Maggie's seance *could* have been a useful way of sussing me out. But everybody knows me anyway. Ten minutes in Woody's nosh bar would have done as well. Unless they really did believe this seance stuff? That at least would explain why Owd Maggie was done in. But there was something missing. And I had a feeling that Donna Vernon didn't believe this seance stuff any more than me.

Then there was Pearlhanger.

Names have a ring to them, don't they? A curious atmosphere even though you've never seen the place.

Pearl as in pearl, but hanger in the old speech means a steep wood, a loop of dress, a belt, or an ancient short sword. There's a sea-village not far off called Goldhanger, named for where a gold-handled sword was found centuries ago. The same must have been for Pearlhanger. We got a lot of marauders in olden days, tourists' ancient forerunners. The famed Battle of Maldon was on this coast, and the treasure of the Viking king at Sutton Hoo. It's a universal law that warriors get gold. For gold read gems, diamonds, silver.

And pearls.

Pearls have magic in them, simply because there's no such thing as an 'ordinary' pearl. Each one seems to have a right to legend. Coco Chanel—yes, *that* one—once heaved a perfect pearl necklace into the briny, displeased at Bendor Grosvenor, Duke of Westminster. Aren't women odd? All because he'd done a little two-timing. Well, sixty-five timing. But ditching a priceless necklace of gemstones in a temper is still basically an unreasonable act. Adverts for Chanel No. 5 make me wince at that memory. But then, a grandad's age ago, Kentucky anglers used to chuck freshwater pearls back in the river if they hooked a mussel by mistake.

Funny thing, but some gems—and the pearl is a classified gemstone, remember—are special. They appeal to something in the mind. The pearl is one. Passion and ignorance have haunted it. Like the Inca of Peru used to cook oysters just to extract the pearl. I ask you. And Sir Thomas Gresham drank Queen Bess's health in wine containing pearl-powder made by grinding up a huge and precious pearl. Well, Sir Thomas was only doing what Cleopatra and Clodius the famous Roman glutton used to do. Celtic freshwater pearls, and oyster pearls from the untended Roman oyster beds, were always desirable. There seems to have been plenty knocking around in those days, enough to cause the Paris goldsmiths in 1355 to forbid 'setting Scotch pearls with the Oriental'. Long before that the Egyptians thrived as middlemen between Rome and the ancient Macedonians' pearl fisheries in the Red Sea. You see how romance and pearls go together? But it's often romance of a peculiar and oddly rather sinister kind. Like, you can't call Caligula's huge pearl necklace romantic, because it was for his favourite horse. And his wife Lollia Paulina's craving for pearls was too passionate for sanity, though that was par for the course in Caligula's household. They were all loony.

Men wore them too, hung as a little clapper in a tiny gold bell earring. It became such a craze that Cæsar put a stop to these *crotalia*, little rattles, because unmarried women were wearing them as a sexy invitation. Some say that Julius Cæsar invaded us simply to capture the Old World's best source of freshwater pearls.

I returned the hire car about two in the morning. The night man drove me to the inn. He was grinning. 'Lot of business at the Drum and Fife tonight. My brother dropped a fare here not ten minutes gone.'

'You jest,' I said, but feeling odd.

'Straight up.' He grinned even wider. 'Be funny if it wuz your missus, eh?'

'Hilarious,' I agreed, and stealthily climbed the stairs. No light under Donna's door. Life was becoming a Restoration comedy without the laughs.

Badly knackered though I was, sleep was long coming.

I'd worked out everything for Lydia to do and told her on the blower. Now I wanted Tinker, please God, to be waiting somewhere handy down Salcott. I wanted Lydia to have made the right contacts. I wanted Beatrice to arrange a seance to contact Owd Maggie, RIP. I wanted Mel and Sandy to get a move on. I wanted to catch Sid Vernon and his crooked mate, Chatto, and I wanted Ledger to lay aside the *Sporting Chronicle* and arrest the pair of them. I wanted Donna.

Did I mean Margaret? Helen? Lydia? Must have done . . .

'Two more,' Donna said. 'Then the last. We'll catch Sid up at the speed we're going.' She said it like a line from a play. Odd how often that thought recurred.

'No real hurry now, is there?' I was all innocence. She'd let me drive. There was an end-of-term air about. 'He's spent nothing. So your savings will be intact.'

She remembered to nod. 'It's that policeman, and the other man he mentioned. Whatever was he called?' Another line, quite well spoken.

'Kenneth W. Chatto,' I said, 'I think.' Her husband's partner, and she's pretending she didn't know his name.

'Only, they assumed he was some sort of crook.'

I tut-tutted. 'Terrible. They'll forget. Police always do.'

They might, but not me.

That morning I bombed us through the remnants of the antiques sweep like a blue-bummed electron. They were easy, the way everything is when you're sure of yourself and stupid. One was a councillor living up to his principles by flogging grotty junk to the electorate in support of social equality, which includes his ten-acre mansion, and his dark-haired mistress. (She's secret; lives on the left, first floor, that steep road going up from the river in Maldon, Essex.) I don't have much truck with George's sincere principles because all politicians are failed people. They have a right to expect exactly the same sincerity and care they give us, so I felt absolved of morality. I knew him of old, and actually laughed aloud at the reproduction cabinet he showed us, most sincerely of course. Fakes are his hobby.

'You bloody fool, George. You didn't even make it out of an *old* wardrobe. And a genuine china cabinet has two different heights, shelves on top behind glass and a cupboard underneath. You've made the sides from one slab, frigging nerk.'

'That other dealer liked it, Lovejoy.'

'Vernon? Did he buy it?'

George shook his head glumly. 'Short of cash.'

Maybe Vernon wasn't so thick after all. 'Look, George.' I couldn't resist pointing out the astragal bars, the wood lattice he'd put across the glass. 'You must dovetail astragals into the bloody frame, not just stick the glass in with putty.'

'I mixed the putty with dust,' he defended.

Honest to God. 'You nerk. And old glass must warp outwards. It can be done quite easily—'

'Don't be narked, Lovejoy . . .'

I gave up and left. Even a faker has a right to life.

'No good,' I told Donna, getting in the car. 'Just a politician redistributing wealth.' I leant across and called up, 'Regards to Pat, George. Hope her leg's better.'

'Shhh,' he was saying desperately, glancing furtively into the house in case his wife heard.

We'd done the second call by eleven. I'd got going again. If I hadn't been so conscientious we'd have been late for the murder, but how was I to know I should have been thinking ahead? Anyway it too was a fake, though you could have guessed that from the *Advertiser*'s description of a genuine set of fretwork mahogany wall shelves 'by Chippendale'. Old John Tansby makes these down in Colchester, and he's never forged a set right yet. I've told him a million times that Chippendale hated leaving round corners on his fret and insisted they be filed square, but you might as well talk to the wall. I ask you. What chance has an honest fake got?

All the way to last call—Salcott—I chatted about antiques, fakes, twinned bureaux, crass 'marry-ups' (posh books call them 'marriages', but nobody living uses the word) made from two dissimilar chunks of genuine pieces. I didn't stop talking, even made Donna laugh. I felt great. She looked lovely, breeze blowing her bright hair and her pretty face free of that metallic look she'd once had. A pleasant ride.

The motor halted of its own accord on a raised brow. We scanned over sea marshes, a few houseboats of all shapes and colours on the mudflats, colourful sails slowly sweeping the reedy bay. A low creek gleamed to our right with a few whitewashed cottages in a row marking the end of Salcott. A cluster of houses formed a small harbour. A pub's sign swung the sun's reflection at us, flash, flash.

'End of the road, Donna.' I consulted my list. 'Antique brooch. A Mr Deamer.'

'Pretty little place,' she said, straight out of summer rep.

'Isn't it?' I agreed, and decided to try it out. I'd been saving it up. 'Pearlhanger, locals still call that end stretch.'

'Do they really?' she replied evenly.

We drove down and booked in at the one tavern. Tinker was getting pickled in the taproom. He saw us come but didn't call hello, as instructed. I carried our bags up to our rooms, thanking my lucky stars that something was going right at last.

Pearlhanger. They'd be here.

CHAPTER 14

Deamer, when we finally reached his vast rambling house out on a small peninsula, was an angular warped old gentle-

man scholar, all wheezes, with tufts of hair sprouting sideways from all round his head. The effect was monastic. He'd
be sure to get credit from tradespeople.

'Do come in,' he gasped, shuffling ahead of us. 'I don't
get many visitors these days.' So? We closed the door and
followed. Tiled floors, echoes. A barn of a place with the
old sprung bells still glimpsed down the servants' hallway
for indicating which room had fallen into thirst.

'We came,' I said in procession to his rocking kyphosis,
'on account of—'

'The other gentleman's just deciding,' Mr Deamer quavered. We angled into a passageway lined one side by stained
glass. A glassed-in cloister. You know, a Victorian house
really has quality. The corridor's wooden panels were delectable, the lintels matured and the ceiling plaster could have
been laid yesterday—correction: no, it couldn't; modern
stuff'd have fallen off. 'In the withdrawing-room. Do please
enter.'

We entered and there stood a vaguely familiar man,
lanky-tall, close-cropped hair, still that tatty anorak. We
faced each other like scruffy book-ends. He was examining
a pendant.

'Hello again,' I said. 'Lovejoy. Mrs Donna Vernon.'

'Smethurst,' he said. 'Again? I don't recall . . .'

'We bumped into you in Jackson's restaurant.'

'Oh. Sorry. Mmmmh.' He turned to the old man. 'I'll
take it. At the price you asked.'

'Splendid, splendid.'

We all paused. Now, two small points. Antique dealers,
collectors, *nobody* pays an asking price just like that. And my
chest had not even clanged a single chime. If the brooch
was any sort of antique I'd have felt at least a dong. Well,
I wasn't going to argue over a crummy modern piece of
jeweller's tat, valuable or not.

'Look, dad,' I said to break the deadlock. 'Can I use your
loo?'

Gracious permission received, I roamed away from that strange tableau and sure enough was delighted to find a valuable collectible. Lavatory-collecting might sound a bit eclectic, but you can make fortunes from this prestigious artform. It was a real joy, an item to be used with respect. You yank on a handle to work the valve. To my delight it had the now renowned Looking Glass Bottom Valve. Pontifex made these during the 1890s in London's Shoe Lane, presumably for folk with complicated ailments. Not bad for five bob, which is what they cost then. Nice glaze, and three lots of floral decoration in blue, set in best carved beechwood.

They had moved apart when I returned. 'Great loo, dad,' I told old Deamer. 'If you want to sell it, let me know. Incidentally, has a Sid Vernon called?'

'No,' Donna said for him. 'I've already asked.'

'If he does,' I said to the old scholar, 'we'll be waiting for him at the tavern. All right?'

Donna stirred with exasperation. 'Have a look, Lovejoy.'

'Eh? Oh.' I had a casual glance, a nice piece of goldsmithing round a fair-sized baroque pearl. You have to grin sometimes. It wasn't bad. The big baroque's shape had been used to form the busty torso of a siren. Yet another phoney siren pendant. Oh, it was all there: small baroque pearls hanging from her fish-tailed body, a modern synthetic diamond for her mirror, two little seed pearls under her arm the way you carry a ball. It even had 'VD' stamped on, like the proper Siren. I handed it back. You see all sorts of copies once an antique gets its photo in the papers.

'Great,' I said absently.

Deamer rang the bell-pull. An aged crone came to walk us to the door. Donna hung back making unnecessarily effusive thanks, I thought, to Mr Deamer. I was plodding ahead with the housekeeper, asking her about the house, so took no notice.

We drove down to the creek quite contentedly, me ex-

plaining as I drove the saga of the Canning Siren. 'Lots of
copies are made,' I told Donna, but being careful. 'Every
famous jewel, antique, painting, has its phoneys. Why,' I
chuckled, not watching her face, 'there was rumour of a
Siren variant some idiots were trying to sell only a year or
so back. A laugh, really.' I thought Smethurst a plant, a
deliberate ally of Sid Vernon and his elusive partner Chatto.

She waited silently as I parked beside the inn's green-
sward. A few old geezers were taking the air in the watery
sun, swilling ale.

'Right. That's it, then.' I was poisonously hearty. 'All
done. Over and out. We've obviously overtaken him on the
way.'

Donna was still. 'Thank you, then, Lovejoy.'

'You'll settle up with Lydia, right? I don't like asking,
but she's a stickler for details. I can get a lift back.'

'Lovejoy.'

'Yes?' I'd been getting out. Her voice made me sit for
more.

She spoke unlooking, in a low voice. 'In all these days
you've behaved abominably. That tarty bitch Michaela
French. You were definitely crumpled returning from Mrs
Sutton's. That slatternly Mrs Smith, the one you tried to
make do my hair. You've ogled and drooled over them all.
Even that mare in the homemade caftan.' She meant the
yoghurt girl with the screen-printer. 'I could tell you were
a chauvinist swine, with that Beatrice drunkard by the
harbour. And your tame mousey apprentice.'

'Hand on my heart, Donna,' I tried. 'I—'

She was looking steadfastly out through the windscreen.
'What's wrong with me, Lovejoy?'

'Eh?'

'All this time. Staying in the same places, travelling
together, everything shared. And you've never once . . .
What's wrong?'

'Er, well,' I said, thinking fast. 'You're, er . . .' Telling her she seemed like an ironclad was probably more imperialism.

She leant across and, in full view of the toothy old sods on the pub bench, she put her warm dry mouth on mine. She even began to stroke me. Broad daylight, among a yachting crowd. A cheer went up from a quartet of young suntanned arrivals crossing into the saloon bar.

'Here, nark it.' I pulled away, red-faced. This must be how women feel.

Eventually we went in, me sheepishly trying to avoid the old blokes' wrinkled faces.

What happened then was inevitable, really. We were discreet, didn't make a lot of noise I don't suppose, and Donna pulled the curtains even though it only overlooked upstream where the yachts never bother going. She was a fury, lovely and exhilarating. It's always the same, naturally, but she seemed fuelled by that berserk wanton energy which is wonderful to experience at the time yet leaves you wondering what it was all about. Silly to dwell on it, I told myself while she knelt beside me afterwards and soaped me in the bath, because love's love and not to be questioned. She was laughing, really laughing, with a delicious merriment I never thought she was capable of. I've always been convinced that love is its own self, that love is simply making love, no matter where or when. That afternoon Donna Vernon made it seem a delirious gallop.

Love-hunger takes a zillion forms. It can appear as plain honest greed, religious mysticism or bobby-dazzling creativity, but it's bingo every time. No mistake. Pretend it's belly-ache for all you're worth, but you know and she knows there'll be no peace until you-know-what. Over the years I've evolved this philosophy to cope with it: give in. Surrender your honour and virtue. Let guilt go hang. People keep saying it's wrong but I ask straight out: Why? and they've never any answer worth half an ear. This is why cynics have a hard time; longing and bitterness can't last.

As the tavern quietened in the afternoon lull, we slept.

At six o'clock we went down and had our nosh in the dining-room. We had a walk. You won't believe this, but I even shook my head when Tinker signalled me. He shrugged and went back to his ale.

All right, I admit I was besotted. Common sense and reason had left my thick skull. It came on coolish with a breeze about ten o'clock. Still no sign of Vernon. Donna, bless her thoughtful heart, suggested we go in separately so as to avoid scandal.

'Give me ten minutes, darling,' she said, and walked along the hard to the tavern. I waited before the old creek cottages for her footsteps to recede and watched the sea's reflected lights.

These cottages are mostly derelict now. They were once inhabited, eelers, fishermen, wherrymen, coastguards, those estuary folk. It's becoming the fashion to buy them up as holiday homes, and a couple were showing signs of repair. The rest are used as doss-houses by anybody as takes a fancy.

Ten minutes, give or take a yard. I strolled in to the tavern, called a cheery good night to the landlord and went upstairs.

She welcomed me in furnace heat. For an hour or so we made love with silent intensity and slept. Some time in the dark hours Donna woke me and said I'd best go back to my own room.

One of the unwritten laws, I suppose, is that women have the final say in these matters. Another torrid session and I was creeping off across the corridor with all the stealth of which I am capable, which is a very great deal.

Then I slept the sleep of the just. Do no harm to stay around a day or three with the delectable Donna. Vaguely I wondered if I was a tax-deductible expense.

At six o'clock in the morning I was wakened by Ledger, who arrested me for the murder of Sidney Charles Vernon, antique dealer. He didn't even bring a cup of tea, which was unfair. You get that even in gaol.

CHAPTER 15

It's queer when you think of it, what a crowd-puller murder is. I mean, there was Salcott, population a sparse 219 souls in the breeding season, suddenly disgorging a throng which covered every boggy nook and cranny of the estuary. They floated a flotilla of dinghies to get a better view. Normally this performance is reserved for Armadas.

'What's it about, Ledger?' The bastard'd hardly given me time to dress.

'You heard, lad. You're for it.'

'Murder? Straight up?'

We were trudging along the hard ogled by the silent horde. Funny again, but there was that intense blond bloke in his mac among the mob. Ledger stopped suddenly. Followers dominoed up against us, bloody fools. People should watch where they're going. A bloke could be pushed over the side and tumble down . . . down to lie on the pebbly mud below exactly where a bloke's body lay right now. Between the salt water and the sea sand. His head was crumpled, looking like wrinkled crêpe paper before it gets pulled tight. An eel was coiled nearby, its disgusting tyre-thickness fatter than eels have a right to be. I felt sick.

We were outside the derelict cottages. A tired rivulet ran below a small hooped bridge under the footpath. It was where I'd waited last night before following Donna in for our last bout of fervid passion.

'Smethurst,' I said, craning my head round to align better on his face.

'It's nobody called Smethurst, Lovejoy. You've killed Sidney Charles Vernon.'

'That's Smethurst. He told me so himself.'

'We'll ask the judge,' Ledger said. 'He'll know. All right,

lads,' he called to sundry plainclothes peelers and bobbies
nodding off among the foliage. 'Wrap it up. Where's the
local?'

'Me, sir,' offered a uniformed bloke. He was so deliriously
happy all this was happening on his very own manor that
I'd have tagged him for chief suspect. 'I've already got
statements from the kiddies who found him. I've sent for
their parents.'

Three white-faced lads about seven years old were being
awestruck nearby. They had little spades and a bucket. Out
early digging lugworms for fishing. No wonder there's all
this violence about when they start massacres that young.

We made the nick in record time. Sirens and lights,
bullying shouts, all the general hysteria of which only
psychopaths are capable. You can easily see how warped
personalities become addicted to the robber-baron life style.
I was still feeling superior when they sat me opposite Ledger
and four scribblers.

Donna came in, so white she was almost transparent, but
calm. Why calm, for Christ's sake? She didn't look at me.
And the publican and his girls from the Welcome Sailor
where we'd stayed at Salcott. Last but not least, old Mr
Deamer came in sounding like confetti with asthma.

My superior feelings fell away. Headache time. Plans
were going wrong, all of them mine.

They took my statement first. I gave them almost all of
it: the seance, Donna's hiring arrangement, Beatrice, the
sweep—here I shakily produced my copy of the list, as if it
made me saintly—and finally running into Smethurst at Mr
Deamer's old house. I included approximate details of Mel
and Sandy, and Tinker.

'You saw Vernon in possession of a valuable antique
pendant, of a type similar to a more famous one?'

'No. I saw Smethurst buy a Siren fake from Mr Deamer.'
I smiled encouragingly at Deamer and gave him a wink.

Soon he'd scupper all this. 'Vernon wasn't there. Donna
will tell you.'

Donna said nothing. She looked at the floor, pale and
interesting. During my statement she had asked for a glass
of water which a policewoman brought her with a glare at
me.

'Then?' Ledger said. His expression said, *Got you!*

'Donna, er, Mrs Vernon and I went back to the tavern,
had a rest, supper, and, er, retired.'

He asked me details of times and whatnot. I signed the
typescript with a wobbly flourish. We fell quiet.

'This is what we think really happened, Lovejoy: yesterday you arrived at Mr Deamer's house in company with
Mrs Vernon. You'd finally caught up with Sidney Vernon.
You made an offer for the antique pearl pendant, pretending
it was a mere replica to deceive the elderly owner.'

'Here. That's the wrong way about—'

'Shut it, Lovejoy. Once your clumsy purchase attempt
failed, you waylaid Vernon outside the cottages in the
darkness, demanding the pendant. And he died, Lovejoy.'

I glanced from Donna to old Deamer. They were looking
sober and old Deamer was nodding affirmatively at all this
crap. 'Here,' I said. I was in one of those static sweats you
get in a trap.

'On the way out of Mr Deamer's you closely questioned
the elderly housekeeper as to the layout of the dwelling?'

'Well, in a way, yes,' I said weakly.

'You arrived at the Welcome Sailor, where six old fishermen saw you forcing your attentions on Mrs Vernon in the
car. During the evening you again accosted her. She returned to the tavern alone at ten o'clock. Having ascertained
from her that the antique was still in Vernon's possession,
you assaulted Vernon, removed the desired object, put it in
an envelope addressed to your own cottage, and posted it
in the Salcott pillarbox.'

Ledger pulled out the gungey baroque-pearl pendant. Still

fake. 'This was recovered from such an envelope, Lovejoy. It bears your fingerprints.'

'Police aren't allowed to tamper with the Royal Mail, Ledger.' Donna still said nothing. Lost, I quavered, 'No. You see, Donna didn't, er . . .'

'Reject your unwelcome attentions, Lovejoy? Then why did she rouse the landlord and seek refuge with him and his family at three-thirty a.m.?'

I piped, 'Donna? For Christ's sake.'

'Your account is true, Sergeant,' Donna said softly, and was assisted out of the room. Another exit line, I supposed. That summer rep feeling had been justified.

'Look, Ledger. I wouldn't do a bloke in for a dud.'

'Real gold. Real pearls, Lovejoy.' He made a gesture of levitation. 'You can all go. Thank you for your cooperation.' He smiled at me. 'Not you, Lovejoy.'

My new cell was same as always. Same niff. Same screw with a million jokes about bars, keys, magistrates and crimes. A real laugh. Same graffiti, same old hat, one witty line.

Donna hadn't wanted me to leave. Hence the torrid love. And Sid Vernon was in on her scam, hence all the deception at old Deamer's house. And Mr Deamer himself was another accomplice, or he wouldn't have lied in his gums just now. Dear God, who wasn't?

CHAPTER 16

Maybe I'd dozed. There was a newspaper but I make up my own lies so I just lay there. Sometimes it seems that, however brightly a day begins, it ends with a choice of degradations. There was nothing going for me except inno-cence—good for a laugh, though they say it counts in heaven.

You always get death on a coast. It doesn't have to be

a Bermuda Triangle. Accidents happen. But presumably
Ledger had found some blunt instrument? It wasn't much
of a tumble for Vernon, the few feet down from the path,
and mud's soft. Add this to Donna's bewildering behaviour
and . . .

'You're sprung, Lovejoy. Out of it.'

Harder to wake up into daytime than night, and relief is
hard any old time. The constable thumbed me down the
corridor. They're not allowed to touch you—another guf-
faw—so he could only glower hatred as I emerged, blinking.

'Good morning, Lovejoy.' Lydia stood there. High-
throated lace blouse, smart blue suit, seamed stockings and
strap heels. A goddess to the rescue. 'Constable,' she was
saying severely to the desk sergeant, 'I want to complain.
Lovejoy hasn't shaved.'

Tinker was snoring on the bench. A young couple huddled
like kipping hamsters.

'Er, look,' I said in a panic, thinking: Christ. This just
wasn't the time.

The sergeant had had enough. Rolling his eyes at me, he
made me sign that I'd got all my things.

'Is this why we pay our taxes?' Lydia was demanding as
I bundled her out, hauling Tinker as I went. 'This behoves
a letter to our Member of Parliament—'

We didn't stop until I reached the corner by the old flax
house. Lydia was still seething and behoving. The pub
wasn't open so we sat on the memorial bench, safe among
noise and shoppers and traffic. Bliss. I put my head back.
You know that feeling when you've been through the
mangle?

Lydia told me how Tinker had seen me and Donna talking
by the creek cottages. 'I went down earlier to visit Tinker
because he seemed so lonely on his own. I took him some
things, made him comfortable.'

'Ledger took Tinker's word that I'd left there without
seeing Vernon?'

'No, Lovejoy. Tinker'd actually let part of the cottage off to two young campers. Very reprehensible—it isn't his property—but fortunate in the circumstances. They also saw you and were able to corroborate—'

By a whisker. 'Good old Tinker.'

'But furthermore, Lovejoy,' she said portentously through Tinker's snores as the traffic hurtled and surviving pedestrians shuffled. 'I have something to say.'

Dear God no, I thought. Not now. She's going to say this is all too much. Laying about with Donna, murder charges. I wanted to crawl into a hole. What a frigging world. Everybody corrupt with rotten self-seeking.

'Go on,' I said dully.

'It's . . . it's money.'

That really made me rouse and stare. 'Eh?'

She faced me on the bench. People milled by. Tinker snored.

'Do you know how much I paid yesterday for mushrooms, Lovejoy?' She clasped her hands on her lap.

'Er,' I said, fascinated in spite of myself.

'They've gone up five pence, Lovejoy. Now, as you well know, I'm not one to complain, but . . .'

She'd made a list of commodities, foods and whatnots, to prove Lovejoy Antiques Inc. wasn't making enough gelt. It came from her handbag like a roll of wallpaper, endless and wide. I closed my eyes, suddenly weak. She rabbited on and on. That's all it was, her bloody wage. I hadn't paid her for months anyway.

'Which is why,' she explained, trying to be casual, 'I've drawn out my savings.' She delved and gave me a cheque. 'Please regard it as a loan only. Until this terrible business is over.'

The words blurred on the cheque for a minute. I looked away. Isn't it a good world? People are really generous and far-seeing deep down. It's only perceptive souls like me that recognize people's true worth. Money can't be bought.

'And,' Lydia said, 'I've sent for the two, ah, boys. We need all the help—'

Several motorhorns sounded. A falsetto screeched, 'Lovejoy!' I prayed again, but it was. The Rover of many colours. Heaven knows what it is about me, but I've never had a prayer answered yet.

'Lovejoy!' Sandy marched—well, minced—across the crowded pavement and stood, hand on hip, fluorescent copper-blue handbag swinging. 'Your sweep what an absolute tremenduloso I mean *what a fiasco!*' He plumped on the seat and gazed ardently into his reflection. He has tiny gilt mirrors on his gloves. I suppose I must have been a rotter in some earlier existence.

'Er, Sandy. Your motor . . .' He'd parked it on the High Street's one pedestrian crossing. Mel sat stony-faced in the passenger seat. Another row.

'Oh, you *noticed!*' Sandy rose, did a little skip and cried, 'Mel, dear! Lovejoy *adores* the new wings.' He whispered to me, '*Tell* him, Lovejoy! He's in rather a *mood.*'

'Er,' I said nervously. 'They're, er, great, Mel.'

The big old Rover was now adorned with two white metal wings projecting from the mudguards. Not, note, wings as in car, but as in angel. It was bloody daft.

Mel glanced across. 'Do you, Lovejoy?'

'Really, Lovejoy?' Lydia said doubtfully, eyeing the car. 'White's such a risk.'

'Well, dearie,' Sandy trilled venomously at her. 'We all *know* where *your* colour sense goes in the winter time don't we I mean can we ever *forgive* that opal *harness* you wore over that plastic last Easter *oooh!*'

His screech made me leap a mile. Every head turned. He was pointing dramatically at Lydia's face. 'You got it! Mel, dear. Come and *see!* Lydia's got that new flickershade eye lustre *oooh!*'

I thought: Honest to God I can't stand much more. I'd just escaped the scaffold.

Mel descended. 'Lovely, dear,' he said sweetly. 'Let's hope you learn how to use it. The fashion might come back. One day.'

'Whose car's that?' A traffic warden, all I needed.

'Ours, dear,' Sandy said. 'D'you want a ride?'

'What the fuck's it doing parked at traffic lights?'

Sandy tittered. 'Red and amber go with it, sweetie-pie. But your *green*!'

'Right.' He pulled out his notepad, paused, looked at me. 'Here. You the bloke as got done for murder?'

'Murder?' Sandy screamed, faked a dramatic swoon. 'Whose?'

'Mr Vernon's,' Lydia said. 'But it was a false charge—'

'Oh, *him*! Is that all?' Sandy ostentatiously returned his smelling salts to his handbag with a relieved flourish.

'Right. I'm booking the lot of you,' from the threatening warden.

'You know Vernon, Sandy?' I asked.

'Oooh, I love macho!' Sandy squealed. He stepped forward and gazed soulfully into the goon's eyes. '*Promise* you'll take my phone number, dear?'

'And Chatto,' Mel said. 'He lodges with Deamer. They own that riverside estate down Salcott. His hair's quite wrong, of course.'

'Fancy that,' I said faintly, thinking. So Chatto stayed with Deamer. No wonder it had all been so easy for them to plan. The low spit of land on which Deamer's house stood rose into my mind.

'I love uniforms.' Sandy's hand was looped in the goon's belt. The idiot, scarlet with embarrassment, escaped. Sandy's voice rose to a penetrating falsetto. '*Must* you go, dear? You can play with the gear stick . . .' People were smiling. Everybody knows Sandy and Mel. They've got out of more scrapes than Pearl White. This was just Sandy's technique.

Abruptly I was on my feet, looking at them. My resources.

Two oddities, a drunken barker, a specky prim bird hooked on health foods and properly aired underwear, and me. Still, it was the only army I'd got.

'Look, troops,' I said. 'Where'll I get an aeroplane?'

'That Cow Vanessa,' Sandy said absently, doing his eyes. 'If you like blue.'

We left Tinker and Lydia. They drove me off, arguing about their new fibre optic screen wipers ('But, Mel, how else can we wave at friends?' from Sandy). I tried explaining that I wanted to land secretly near Deamer's mansion house and burgle the place to see who'd murdered Donna's husband and Owd Maggie and bubbled me to be hanged, and find out who was pulling a pearl scam. Surely it wasn't too much to ask? They didn't really listen.

'That peroxide bitch is behind it all,' Mel said.

Sandy tittered. 'Dear Donna wears such *canopies* over those *gaswork* hips I mean she could be hiding *anyone*!'

'You know Donna too, Sandy?' I asked.

'Doesn't everyone, cherub? I told her the other week at Madame Blavatsky's you remember Mel I had *fits* over her coral-red shoes—'

'Walter has a plane,' Mel cut in. 'Let's try him. He flies really well.'

'Only when he smokes those strange powders, dear,' Sandy said, giggling.

My headache was back. 'Sandy,' I got out. 'Donna Vernon.'

Sandy had his powder compact out. 'Desperate Donna poor hag calling up all *possible* supernatural forces!' I tried to get a word in edgeways because there were a million clues here in full flight.

'Don't mock the afflicted, Sandy dear,' from Mel.

Sandy giggled. 'Mel's furious because he took a shine to her fancyman with the curls. Groper Chatto, poor lamb. A mystery, Lovejoy. She's so *plain*.'

This morning with the police Donna had looked quite distracted. No wonder she'd not realized the danger I was in on account of her testimony. She was only in Chatto's scam because she was coerced. That was transparently plain. If Deamer and Chatto came croppers in the process it'd just be their hard luck. Well, whatever happened I'd still be the same shape in the bath tomorrow.

'Wake me when we're there,' I said, and nodded off, bushed.

CHAPTER 17

Dolly, that I knew once, used to say that my lifestyle was an embarrassment. In fact it's the other way about: embarrassment's my lifestyle.

Luckily Boxenford's remote, one of those flattish areas of East Anglia where squadrons were stationed during the war. Occasionally our local paper carries pictures of American veterans returning to see how far downhill it's gone since they left.

Airports don't bring out the best in me. I dislike them—correction: I hate them. I always get a wheelie that wants to go anticlockwise and the tickets are baffling. Other civilizations left Lindisfarne Gospels. We'll leave a Dan-Air counterfoil. Airports to me mean spewing tots, and blotch-faced sleepless aunties plodding between loos and the duty-free. Airports are anonymous hotels, Levantine staff in brown and maroon talking Peter Lorre English, croissants instead of breakfast, and only the hotel flag logo ever changes. Travel used to mean the joyous experience of places. Once.

'We're here, Lovejoy.'

Rousing, I looked out. The harbour. We were outside Beatrice's cottage. 'What's going on?' I asked.

'Time for your seance, Lovejoy,' Sandy said. 'Mel will fix your flight with That Cow Vanessa while you're at it.'

'Give Cardew my regards,' Mel said. 'He's nice.'

It's women, not men, who go for mystery, not to mention mystique. They're hooked on Meanings and What's Foretold and all that jazz. You can't blame them, I suppose. Nothing else to do all day. They've got to fill their time somehow.

Once, I knew this bouncy dark-haired bird Angelina who was a zodiacal astrologist, whatever that is. Her bed crawled with embroidered signs. She ran her life to a starry timetable that had no relationship with Planet Earth or us inhabitants. Some days were great for this or that. Others were death. Oh, I'm not knocking it. Don't get me wrong. There's this London professor (though only psychology, so maybe he's a nut too) who's proved all Olympic gold-medallists are Aries or something. And women's magazines are full of it. I'm simply open-minded, even about rubbish as long as there's gelt to be made out of it. Anyway, this bird Angelina was a raving, er, friend. We'd met doing battle over a Cromwellian chair—solid square panel back, arms dead horizontal, legs bobbin-turned, brass-nailed leather covering the seat and back. (All those romantic movies are wrong, showing people sitting on chairs when they should be on stools; stools were twenty times as common.) Angelina outbid me. 'It was in my prediction for today,' she told me afterwards. We were enthusiastic friends for two months, then she discovered that she'd misread our horoscopes and gave me the push. Apparently we'd been erroneously enjoying incompatibility all along. I've not forgiven her that chair, though. I never did get it.

What I mean is that the future's guesswork, isn't it? Otherwise it wouldn't be future. So, while futurists might be really brimful of worthwhile data, the rest of us wait disbelievingly for a translation.

And don't think there was any significance in that odd line from the old folk tune, between the salt water and the sea sand. Songs aren't psychic. You'd go off your head if you let coincidences worry you. I was only after proof that Chatto'd killed Owd Maggie and Sid Vernon to liberate my lovely Donna. Anybody who knows me will swear I'm not given to vengeance. I was only after justice. Honest truth.

Keeping calm, I went in. Mel had wanted to come too but Sandy wouldn't let him. Barney was out piloting the ocean wave. Beatrice was there, Sandy, me, that plump middle-aged bird I'd liked at Owd Maggie's seance, her dried-prune husband, two nondescript grannies, and a serious old bald geezer who had to contemplate alone for a few minutes before the whistle. Bea told me she'd brought her friend Seth, but I was damned if I could see him. There were eight chairs.

'Does it have to be so hot in here?'

'Shhh, Lovejoy. Don't be afraid,' Beatrice said, patting my hand.

Stupid woman; wrong end of the stick again. Afraid? I ask you. The only thing on my mind was to get the hell out of here and put the finger on Chatto by raiding old Deamer's house ...

'Hands,' the plumpish lady was saying to me. We were supposed to stretch our hands out flat.

'Will it rock about?' I whispered to her. 'Only, on the pictures once—'

'Shhh.'

'Seth,' Beatrice was saying, her eyes closed and breathing rhythmically. We'd all promised to concentrate. Bea's cleavage drew my eyes, honestly accidental. Eyes have got to look somewhere, haven't they? That's their job. The room should have been darkened at least. Or is that for fortune-telling? Faith-healing? 'Seth,' Bea went. 'Please speak to me.'

'Doesn't she mean Cardew?' I whispered.

'Seth is Beatrice's spirit guide. Shhh.'

It was all so mundane. I couldn't imagine anything less
spiritual than a sexy friend tuning in among a motley crew
like us. A right sham. Everybody else was switched on all
right, a picture of concentration. And Bea was doing her
stuff, calling for Seth as if he were an overdue boat on some
distant pleasure-pond. I looked round. The grannies smelled
of lavender mothballs. The plump bird was inflating with
awe while the silence brought out the ticking of her prunish
husband's fob watch. I wondered if it was antique. Baldie
communicated with the Infinite under a frosting of sweat.
It was really gripping, like Wimbledon tennis and telly
cricket, and other interminable yawns. My mind drifted.
Old prints of so-called sports have soared in value. Don't
take any notice of those silly newspaper articles saying half
of the oil paintings in club houses are fakes. Since when did
newspapers ever say anything right about art?

'Do you mean Lovejoy, Seth?' Beatrice said. Nobody had
said anything, not even Seth.

'Here, love,' I said nervously. Well, not nervously, really,
because I'm a cool customer and don't get spooked.

'Shhh,' everybody went, probably Seth as well I shouldn't
wonder.

'Madame Blavatsky, Seth. Is she well?' Bea spoke conversationally, none of that phoney falsetto voice which Owd
Maggie had used.

'Which Madame Blavatsky?' I whispered, and got a
communal ballocking for interrupting. That narked me,
because how can you interrupt a non-conversation?

'Madame is happy, friends,' Beatrice announced, smiling.

Some of us murmured appreciation and relief. I didn't,
though I've nothing really against deception. It's been pretty
useful even to me.

'Seth. Why was Madame struck down?'

This was the crunch. We all saw Beatrice's head nod
to some inner affirmation. Silence. My hands were

damp, but only because it was so damned hot.

'Because of the message,' Beatrice said, as if repeating. 'Seth. Please ask Madame what it was.'

'Look, love,' I whispered to Beatrice while people glared. 'I'll wait outside, have a stroll for a minute.'

I'd risen to leave despite efforts to pull me down. Sweat poured off me. Nothing to do with this farce, of course. Only, the stupid room's heat was practically boiling me alive. The others were simply too stupid to notice it, that's all. Sandy was looking at me, ashen.

'To warn against the death in threes,' Beatrice said in that same unnerving chat-show voice. 'Is the message complete, Seth?'

It frigging well wasn't. 'There were only two deaths,' I croaked.

'A third is near. Friend shall strike friend.'

This was ridiculous. Sweat trickled down my flanks. It stuck in a cold ring round my neck. If I wasn't scared of Barney I'd have given Bea a clout for fooling about like this, because three minus two leaves one.

Their daft game was too much. I had a plane to catch and here I was tarting about while Bea played silly sods.

'Which friend?' I said nastily while the others were being scandalized at my spoiling the show.

Beatrice suddenly opened her eyes, which happened to be fixed straight on me, only pure chance. Owd Maggie's gravelly voice said straight from her mouth, 'Thee, Cocka-lorum.'

CHAPTER 18

Even when I was a virgin—practically before Adam had a lass—I knew that women were born pests. Apart from that brief exhilaration when consummation first equates with life, I've remained pretty well immune to them because I'm reliable, and everybody knows that this quality and women are immiscible, like oil and ale. They have this dyed-in-the-wool knack of nuisance, like horsehair. The old dears who taught me, determined grannies, threatening aunties, lovers, friends, the lot. I'm reasonable and tolerant, and they're not. Simple as that. This incompatibility's bound to cause problems, and invariably I'm the one who comes off worst because fair-minded people always do.

Sandy and Mel drove me back from Beatrice's after I'd developed a bit of a headache at that bloody seance. That's all it was. Everybody gets a headache now and again.

'It was the heat,' I told Lydia for the umpteenth time. They'd collected her on the rainy drive to my cottage.

Sandy was delighted at the rain because his rotating musical wing mirrors had new neon striplights. 'It's your karma, Lovejoy,' he said.

'I hadn't realized Bea could even do impersonations,' I explained. 'Anybody would be shaken, hearing Bea impersonate an old friend who'd pegged out, right?'

Lydia was white as a sheet. I felt mentally spreadeagled.

'Thank you for the journey and your pleasant company, Sandy,' Lydia said formally, hands clasped and feet together. It's her way of saying you can't come in.

'We'll come for you at four, cherubims,' Sandy trilled. 'Today's scoop: watch my rear lights.'

We watched, numbed, as the vast old Rover bowled into the lane. Inevitably two huge red headlamps beamed back at us, the offside dowsing in a horrid slow wink. Even over the motor's din we heard his shrill laughter.

Gone.

Lydia insisted I lie down on the divan while she brewed up. The stunning silence was gradually whittled by normal household sounds. Outside, a bird recovered from Sandy's visit and gave an experimental chirp. Lydia tutted because coat-hangers wouldn't behave when she was tidying. The divan creaked as I turned on my side. A cup chinked. Two garden birds squabbled. A spoon tinked in a saucer. Lydia ahemed for the crunch.

'Lovejoy?'

'Mmmmh?' My eyes were closed against any more shocks.

'How would it be . . . dear,' she managed the endearment with resolve, 'if we asked Constable Ledger for assistance?'

'Why?'

'The police can effect a resolution far more speedily than you alone, Lovejoy.'

She went on in this vein but you can't just lie there taking it.

'Police don't assist. They do what they like.'

'They represent the law, Lovejoy,' the innocent little thing said gravely. Every truth is daft to somebody. I had to explain this.

'Law's trouble for us vulnerables, love. Those who moan hard enough become exempt. Silent folk like you and me get crushed or keep out of its way. The majesty of the law is for those who dispense it.'

Her expression closed into despair, and I knew immediately what she was going to do. Because of Beatrice's silly ventriloquist's trick—ridiculous what grown people will get up to—Lydia was going to phone Ledger. Far more logical to accept that, if I got there quickly and secretly enough, there'd be no third death anyway. Clear as day.

'I am entirely confident,' this endearing little creature said, 'in Vanessa's skills as an aviator. I insisted that Mel ascertain that she is in possession of an authorized pilot-instructress's licence. But your abilities, Lovejoy, cause concern—'

Time to lull suspicions. 'You're probably right, love. Shall I pour?'

At half-three I decided to have a stroll up to the village shop for some envelopes, and put on a great show of being casual. I asked her for some shredded cheese for the robin and chucked it out. Then ostentatiously I ambled up the lane, darted back along the hedge for my bike, and pedalled off like hell towards Boxenford without a single helper, and therefore in a better state of preparedness for survival than I'd been for many a long day.

The plane hadn't arrived when I reached the flying field, two hours later. It looked like no airport I'd ever seen. In a way I was quite glad. Personal service.

Vanessa turned out to be a pleasant lass in oily overalls. She was mending a tiny outboard engine in a shed. A scruffy leather-clad yokel was at a workbench singing to a noisy trannie. A few other blokes were around, one or two busy on other engines. A big kite was laid on the grass. Somebody nearby was using a buzz-saw, judging by the big-wasp sound.

'Wotcher,' I said.

'You Lovejoy?' Vanessa offered me some tinned beer but it always tastes flat as printers' ink. 'Mel says you want to land near that big house beyond Pearlhanger. Between the sea and the sandy spit. That right?'

I avoided her eyes. 'Mmmmh.'

'We've the equipment, if you've the money.'

A pause. I usually try for credit. I've found it goes further. 'What's it cost?'

She smiled, pretty. 'A Japanese helmet, miniature. My brother's an antique dealer in Norwich.'

He would be. 'Fake or genuine?'

'Either.'

'You're on.' Apart from the lacquer it's the cheapest forgery you can do. Starch, shredded paper, sawdust, and that's it. I settled down to wait. A few old posters were fraying on the walls. No hope that they'd be as valuable as the one John Lennon defaced in an American hotel—and which Sotheby's auctioned as Lot 460 for a fortune—but . . .

'Lovejoy?' Vanessa was calling. She was outside, by an

orange sheet fixed to an outboard motor. Pause.

'Yes?' I said. 'Has it arrived?'

The others looked up. Expectancy dwindled, transformed into puzzlement.

'Worried about the wind, mate?' one of the blokes asked kindly. 'You'll be all right. There's hardly a breath.'

They were expecting me to take off. I looked into their seven waiting faces, and Vanessa's brow suddenly cleared. 'Lovejoy. You weren't really expecting an aeroplane? Like a Cessna?' That buzz-saw sounded closer.

I swallowed with difficulty. 'Well, I assumed that flying meant using a frigging plane, love.'

'You're standing on it.' She wasn't without sympathy but inwardly she was rolling about. You can tell. The kind bloke guffawed. The others shook disbelieving heads. I stepped aside. *Plane?*

'Dave's landing one now, Lovejoy.' Vanessa pointed down the field. 'Microlight. Dave can do seventy miles an hour. Some microlights have flown higher than sixteen thousand feet.'

Dave was a distant man-shaped shadow dangling from a noisy orange kite, arriving in the distance with petrifying slowness and at frightening risk. The shadow touched earth, its little legs going like the clappers on the green grass. The engine coughed, spluttered, stopped. I found I'd sat down on the grass. These lunatics weren't aircrew at all. They flew cloth kites, bloody morons.

'Some people are just scared of the idea,' the kindly bloke was saying.

'Here, mate.' Vanessa sacrificed a tin of warmish ale. I sipped while the field settled into place. The intrepid bird-man's figure plodded nearer. The blokes went back to work, one laughing aloud.

'Vanessa, love,' I began, eyeing the wretched thing on the grass beside me. 'There's just no chance of me flying a motorized hankie.'

'Why not?' She was frankly unable to see the problem. 'You just face the breeze and trot forward. Simple as that.'

'Quietness,' I said, delighted at my brilliant mind. 'It has to be silent, you see. Haven't you got a helicopter?'

'You get a hundred decibels of noise even inside a helicopter,' she said scornfully. 'And ninety-six per cent of helicopter pilots get the "leans". And slow-low 'copter flight's famous for its pitch, roll and yaw, as well as its three-axes linear acceleration in controlled hover. In twenty-nine per cent of Royal Navy night hovers over water, disorientation occurred—'

'Great,' I said to stop the flow. Dave merged with the others by the workshed. 'So how do I land without attracting attention on that spit?'

'Hang-glider?' Vanessa suggested. It was no joke. I'd got a serious girl here, though as a salesman she'd starve. I listened dully because you have to humour cranks and women, and she was both. 'The trouble is that up to ten per cent of reported accidents are fatal. Over forty per cent of major injuries are leg fractures, but do keep it all in perspective.'

I'd do that all right. 'In perspective, love,' I said wearily, 'if I won't fly a sodding blanket with an engine you're daft supposing I'll fly one without.'

'You're chicken, Lovejoy.' She was disappointed, shook out her hair like they do. She was politely avoiding saying I'd been brave until I'd realized I wasn't going by Pan-Am.

'There are no windows on the house's top floor that side . . .' I offered.

'Look.' She hesitated, played with a blade of grass to help a thought. 'Lovejoy, can you swim?'

'Yes. But—'

She rose, brushed herself down and, smiling, held out a hand. 'Come on. I'll get you there safely. Cross my heart.' Warily I let her pull me up. An enthusiast's a dangerous creature.

CHAPTER 19

About a million years ago, before funny money and frothy coffee, long before nuns grew legs, folk had reasonable attitudes. Think back. Words were for communication. Gasmen and plumbers turned up. Trains ran with metronomic regularity. A bloke who whined a lot was simply a whiner. Now, his whining means the world has to feel guilty for simply ignoring the miserable so-and-so. Trustworthiness has gone. What I'm on about is that while Vanessa drove us down to Salcott in a toytown motor she gave me her sales talk for Boxenford Flying Club, whose main pursuit seemed to be taking to the air without significant assistance. More odd modern behaviour.

'No, ta,' I said for the umpteenth time. I'd enough trouble on the ground without combing the stratosphere for more.

'You're thinking of accidents,' she urged. 'Don't. They usually happen on landing—sixty-eight per cent—or when taking off, twelve.'

Sixty-eight plus twelve equals eighty, which leaves a measly twenty per cent to survive in. 'No, ta.' Modern means lunatic.

There's a cluster of boat sheds alongside the third ramification of the creek above the point at Pearlhanger. I'd only ever been down there once, and had a hard time remembering where I was. Even as countryside it's dead. There's only these acres of flooded gravel pits where little lads fish and a few apple farms struggle against the North Sea's whippy gales. The trees actually grow bent over, like on moors. A real drag.

Not that it's uninhabited, not like I'm making it sound. Far from it. Hence my need for some form of concealment. Where you get coasts and countryside you'll always find oddities who actually like being there. Bird-watchers hang about, and a few artists dash off occasional masterpieces among the marshes. Speed-boaters race there. Most of the villages have annual regattas. Writers are often swaying about the boozers arguing adverbs.

Vanessa was smiling. 'Now, Lovejoy. I want to say two things. First: I'm the East Coast waterski champion.' Her bad sales tactics were showing. 'Second: trust me.'

Well, yes. As long as she meant trust her with her. Trusting her with me was a different matter.

She drew up near some boat sheds. I followed her down an overgrown path. Most women's bottoms these days are in welded briefs that slice their bums into multiple segments of an arc, four to each cheek. Vanessa's shape was natural. My spirits rose. If she had that degree of innate good sense . . .

'Right, Vanessa,' I said. 'I'll trust you.' For which daftness one hour later I was wobbling on waterskis in a wetsuit like armour. Tenth try without a rest, and I was knackered.

This elderly pipe-smoking man, Tom, steered a small powerboat for me as I floundered on the rope time after stunning time. Vanessa, who had divested with a champion's threatening calm, came with me into the water and kept showing me how. I felt a right prawn and kept begging for a rest.

Tom laughed at me, said I was a sight. Happy as a lawyer at a burial. He hadn't changed, just popped on a bowler hat. I saw with amazement that it actually fitted. Which meant. . .

'Here, Tom,' I puffed, sprawling on the mud. 'Where were you a gamekeeper?' William Coke invented the bowler as protective headgear for gamekeepers on his Norfolk estate. It's really hunting-and-shooting gear. Tom Bowler made the first of these rabbit-fur 'Billy Coke' (hence billy-cock) hats. They still make them the proper way in Stockport, on a potter's wheel and everything, strong enough to

stand on. Labourers all wore them a century ago, the first
ever workers' helmet. Personally marked ones made by
Lock's of St James's are the ones to go for.

'Bowler gave me away, eh?' Tom was saying. 'Here, in
the riverside estate. A mile of banks upstream. Now the
woods are a disgrace. Mr Deamer only thinks of the river,
bad cess to him. Nobody dares go on his stretch any
more.'

Interesting. Vanessa caught my gaze on her. Her face
looked a pure creamy oval in the black suit, a lovely cameo
medallion on an Edwardian lady's elegant black silk dress
. . . Beautiful. She avoided my gaze. I avoided hers.

'Keep trying, Lovejoy,' she said. 'You'll not get near the
house unseen, except on skis. Swim, and the current'll take
you. Sail and they'll see you. We'll waterski you past the
point. You let go. I'll be down in the boat, slip out and
replace you.'

'I realized,' I said huffily. 'I'm not thick.' A little lad was
helping with a long rope, asking Tom for instructions and
calling him Grandad.

We were about two miles from where Deamer's unseen
house stood. To the left, the narrowing river's course. To
the right, the wide estuary and sea beyond with the distant
line of white cottages at Salcott. Tinker was probably in the
boozer by now, lucky lad.

'Right, Lovejoy. Time for work.'

'Your turn,' the kid said. The little psychopath actually
thought I was impatient to have a go. He'd stayed to watch
the show.

'Shut your teeth,' I told him.

'Don't bother Lovejoy, Billy,' Vanessa ordered. 'He's
scared.'

'Sorry, Mum,' the kiddie said. I'm a bit slow sometimes.
My mind was going: If Tom's little Billy's grandad, and
Vanessa's little Billy's mother, then the old ex-gamekeeper
is Vanessa's—The boat jerked me forward so I engulfed a

gallon of estuary. I let go of the rope and floundered.

'No, Lovejoy,' said Billy. 'Point your toes to heaven.'

Six o'clock and the skies darkening. Vanessa had done a last demonstration run. I was a wobbler, but definitely near vertical.

'Time to go now, Lovejoy. Dad'll give you a practice run upriver first as far as the narrows,' Vanessa said, still panting. 'Stay hold of the bar. Lean right back, straighten up as the speed increases.'

'Toes to heaven,' the titch piped.

Disgusted, I grabbed the towbar and stood into the skis. I couldn't look good even to this little lad. He stood on the jetty practising the shoreman's critical gaze.

'Tom,' I bawled. 'Get us out of here, for gawd's sake.'

Vanessa squealed alarm and leapt into the boat. I leaned back, my heart thumping.

'Arms outstretched, toes—'

I said, 'I'll thump you, you little bugger.' The engine growled. Burglary time.

The daylight was fading. I was bruised and my chest was bubbling river water. But I was in there, breathlessly balancing and splashing along on the end of the towbar while the boat ahead created a hell of a disturbance. The problem was the waves which thumped unexpectedly under your feet. Nobody'd warned me about those.

My gaze was on Vanessa, who was applauding and signalling from Tom's boat. She'd never once wavered, always smiling and picking me out of the water whenever I'd floundered, though I think she was less concerned about me than losing the skis.

Vanessa's instructions had been simple. 'Judge the speed, Lovejoy. There's that segment where you can't be seen from the house. When you're in that blind spot, let go of the towbar. Dad will see to direction. You'll keep moving and can wade ashore. Leave the rest to me.'

She ducked down out of sight. Old Tom had this arrangement of mirrors.

For authenticity Vanessa said we would take a wide sweep upriver and then do a long run down, out into the bay and curl in towards the promontory where Deamer's house stood.

The riverbank rises there, half a remote mile inland, where trees crowd down to the water. Engine noise banged back at me from the steeper banks. We came near the narrows. We'd have to turn there or there'd be no more space.

Tom signalled, arm out, and I leaned to take up the curve. Vanessa said some skiers could do it without skis, even, in bare feet . . . To my astonishment I saw a figure standing kneedeep in the river, bent over with his face in a bucket, would you believe. Like children apple-bob, faces in the water. I missed him by a yard, silly sod.

He was suddenly aware of the boat's passing commotion, and wobbled over. I was so startled I yelled out in alarm. The figure wore a tatty overcoat. I was bawling abuse even as I realized it was Tinker. We were past and skittering downstream before I wondered what the hell the stupid goon was up to. Probably drunk as an autumn wasp, as usual. I'd strangle the fool when I got back, frightening me like that.

It was only the coldish wind and spray that was making my teeth chatter. I saw Tom's arm lift and sink, heard the engine rise to a low bellow. The waves beat faster, the rope a taut stick. The motorboat's wake shifted out of my way to a wider angle, thank God. The wooden jetty glided past at some speed, little Billy waving, and we were out into the estuary heading for the bay.

The day was definitely leaning out of the light now. Astonishing how static the whole world seemed. Really weird. The promontory stood there, looming in the fading light. The house was not quite end-on, probably built for views. A distant yacht was moving into the little marina, and one other waterskier was raising a white arc further out than us. Other than that we had clear water. A few cars were switching on their sidelights leaving the marina's car park.

Only the spray proved we were shifting at such speed. The big house turned slowly. Its windows angled, thinned. The blank aspect came wider.

I let go of the bar, kept my angle, slowed and sank gracefully on to sand. A following wave nudged me over, but I didn't mind.

All over bar the shouting.

CHAPTER 20

Before I mutated into an antique dealer I used to have these dreams of suddenly being changed: a dazzling actor, famous explorer, brilliant physicist rising to tumultuous applause to explain his boring new subatomic particle. But I was thankful to wake palpitating into relief, because an actor must know his lines and in my dream I never did. And an explorer has to know how to survive in a blizzard, and I don't. And a physicist must be able to say something to that sea of expectant faces . . . Suddenness, you see, is a killer. Knowledge is the survival factor. Only stupid people find themselves suddenly somewhere, ignorant of what to do.

On my hands and knees without knowing how I'd finished up in that position, and waves splashing gently at my wrists. A dog was watching, crouching breathlessly in hopes of a game. I swore it to boredom and it trotted off, sniffing.

Nothing was broken. I clambered out of my skis and left

the damned things there on the shore. Tom had been right.
He'd bragged he could land me on a tanner, but surely it
was my own brilliance which had glided me to this precise
spot facing Deamer's house's side wall? Anybody would
agree. It's the intrepid young man in his flying machine that
matters. Proudly I unzipped for freer movement. Now a
quick trot over to Deamer's house, grab the evidence that
he and his mate had killed Owd Maggie and Vernon, then
as soon as it was pitch dark cross the tidal path to where
Vanessa would wait with her car as arranged.

Presumably there would be guards around. Silence was
needed. Or was it? Nobody was on guard that I could see.
They could be indoors, or sheltering under the trees, of
course . . . Like a fool, I cleverly decided to outwit them,
and wasted half an hour skulking around outside the house.
By the time I'd got back to my starting place, narked and
scratched and muddy in my underwear, it was completely
dark and I'd not seen or heard a soul. Deamer's mansion
didn't seem guarded at all.

Many oldish houses have a conservatory. They're always
a weak spot, plenty of windows and access through to the
house. I was getting cold. It took me a while to nick some
trellis wire from some plant too bone-idle to stand up on its
own.

Wire goes through putty and round corners. You loosen
the putty then shove the wire through it. Bend the wire to
an angle, direct it into one of the holes so conveniently
punched in the window's handle, and pull. A moment's wait
for a clamour of alarms, then slide yourself in.

Somebody else's house always has a strange feel, so I
stood stock still, letting the lovely old place talk. Quietness
and feelings are the two most underrated commodities these
days—probably because you can't bung them in a bottle
and charge a guinea an ounce.

People were inside. I felt them and the house didn't mind
me. It was safe to move.

The communicating door was unlocked. I remembered that long hallway, the corridor. A feeble seaglow defined the stained-glass window and was reflected back from the delicious old panels. I dropped on all fours and got to the corner. Voices.

People were talking in the study. The old serf had left the light on down the cellar stairs, which was a mercy because enough light cast on the walls and heavy furniture.

'You see, my dear,' Deamer's voice was saying, 'there are risks and risks. Some are unnecessary.'

'And what risk is he?' Donna's voice.

'Pathetically small.'

There was a smile in the old man's voice. I found myself smiling with him. So he too thought little of Ledger. Smugness warmed me. I'd done wonders getting here unseen. A hundred per cent effective. Good old Lovejoy, a real winner. And Donna already here trying to investigate on her own, the dear girl.

'We shouldn't underestimate him,' she said.

A glass chinked. Decanting more sherry, perhaps. I'd love a drop.

'He is a murder suspect, Donna. He has a police record. He has no resources, no finance. Where's the risk?'

Here, I thought, working it out. Hang on.

'I've been with him, Donald. He's erratic, gets distracted by sudden sentiments. Of course he's easily fooled. But there's a streak of violence in Lovejoy that—'

In Lovejoy? Me?

Old Deamer: 'The unfortunate demise of Sidney was necessary when he became so threatening after the event with Mrs Hollohan. Lovejoy is still the prime suspect for both. You agreed at the time, my dear. Don't develop misgivings now.'

Wrong. All this was wrong.

'If it hadn't been for that filthy old man . . .' Donna sounded really regretful. She meant Tinker.

Don't say any more, my mind pleaded with her. The phone rang in the study, very close. I jumped, by a miracle not knocking anything over. Deamer's old man's steps came nearer. I even heard him wheeze. They meant me, me the fool, me not worth a light. And Donna was no poor innocent. She was actually deploring that Tinker had sprung me from the nick when they'd done her husband in.

Deamer was saying calmly, 'And he's what?'

During which pause I felt queasy. Not because all my non-thinking stupidity had finally proved itself, but because I was here high and dry and somebody else was . . .

'Then he has to go, Kenneth,' Deamer said. 'Weren't you supposed to be following Lovejoy?'

Oh Christ. I was sickened. Between the salt water and the sea sand all right.

My dozy cortex yawned itself awake and nudged its alpha rhythms. Ken Chatto had been following me. He knew I was out behind Tom's boat. So why was he now phoning Deamer so urgently? My heart thumped once in fright as realization struck. Tinker.

'Very well.' The receiver went down. A scraping sound, old Deamer laughing. 'Good news, my dear. The old man you detest so much is poaching in the forbidden area. Kenneth is arranging an accident. It will be the usual sort. Two birds with one lucky stone. Marvellous.'

Then Donna said, 'Lovejoy wouldn't go waterskiing, Donald. Never in a million years.' She was thinking, working it out. 'Unless . . .'

I moved, gliding like I'd never done in my life before, out of breath with my heart banging and legs quivering. I fell down that bloody step into the conservatory and scrambled moaning through the window into the fresh dark cold.

Then I ran, down the drive and across the path now flooding ankle-deep in the tide. I didn't even think of sharks and giant sea-monsters. Of course I'd be too late. The knack of idiots.

CHAPTER 21

She was there, bless her, reading—*reading*—a book in the car's interior light when I fell in and gasped for her to drive to the jetty.

'What is it, Lovejoy?'

'Go, *go*!'

You wouldn't think that barely two miles would take an age. My chest was burning and my throat raw. I honestly thought I was dying from panic and effort. That's what comes from being unfit and running blind. Vanessa was pale, driving down this ordinary rural road, peering ahead in the dashboard's glow. A car coming the other way shot past in a dazzle, the crammed occupants singing boisterously. Trees, signposts, coloured bulbs strung across a gate for holiday caravans.

'Sound your horn!' I reached across and pressed on the wheel, blaring the car's horn into the beams. What was SOS? Three longs, three shorts, three longs, or the short blasts first? At least disturb them, tell them I was coming.

'What are we doing, Lovejoy?' She was suddenly scared of me. We'd only known each other for a day. Much I cared, didn't even reply.

We shot down the hedged lanes making a fearsome racket. The occasional strollers now turned to stare. Honestly, I was thinking we'd made it when a maniac white van squeezed terrifyingly past on a narrow bend. I'd cursed it before the significance of its red cross hit me. Hand off the horn then. The blue strobe blinked busily ahead, heeled into the lane leading to the jetty.

'It's an ambulance,' Vanessa said, her face chalk. 'Billy?'

'No. Tinker.'

A vacuum flask and a sandwich box rocked away on the

rear seat. That was a kindness. She was doing me a kindness. I part dressed, grubbily, falling over.

Tinker was being carried into the ambulance when we arrived. The driver had driven through a hedge to reach the jetty and was morosely eyeing the gap for his sedate getaway. A nurse was bullying two blokes to be careful with the stretcher. Tinker looked battered, but his face was uncovered.

'He's still alive,' little Billy complained.

'Tinker. You all right, mate?'

'You're bad news, Lovejoy,' the nerk said. I bent to listen to this abuse. 'A white boat ran into me like you did.'

'Me?' That really narked me. Friends don't strike friends. And I'd actually come to rescue the bad-tempered sod. 'Who were they?'

'They'd have done for me if Tom Connor hadn't happened along, Lovejoy.'

'Leave the patient alone,' the nurse said.

The ambulance driver lit a fag, stared. 'Here,' he said. 'Why've you no socks or shoes on?'

We watched the ambulance crush slowly back through its homemade gap and depart down the track.

'Did you win, Lovejoy?' Vanessa asked. She had her arm through her dad's, from relief.

'At the house? No, love.' I'd lost Donna. I now knew everything but had no proof. Nothing I could do except watch Deamer make a fortune from his scam and see my lovely murderess Donna ride off into the sunset with murderer Chatto to share the spoils. 'Lost everything.'

The sandwiches were still there, and the flask. I brought them across to where Tom and Vanessa were standing, and perched on the edge of the wooden jetty.

'Keep up our strength,' I suggested, unwrapping the grub in the gloaming. 'There are pearls, aren't there? In the river.'

Tom sighed, plumped down with a grunt. Vanessa sat on

her heels, still recovering from her fright. 'How did you know?'

'My superb powers of reason,' I said bitterly. Billy had nicked one of my sandwiches. I pulled the rest closer.

'You nearly took his head off with your skis, Lovejoy,' Tom said. 'I went back to warn him off. It's an unlucky stretch of river, that. A white motor-yacht had clobbered him.'

'Not accidental, I presume.'

Tom shrugged. 'Who knows? I shouted. They took off towards the estuary. I fished Tinker out and raised the alarm.'

'Ta, Tom,' I said.

'Deamer has men all along the banks through his estate, day and night. He says it's to stop anglers after bream, but . . .'

'You do it with a bucket thing, right?'

'Pearl-fishing? Yes. A mask, made out of any old tin. Put leather round the rims, shaped to your face, and bend yourself into the shallow river.'

'Freshwater mussels are secret,' Billy explained. 'Nobody's to tell.'

I said, 'Real pearls? This far south.'

'Them musselbones are here all right,' Tom said. 'Except, ten years ago there was a sudden plenty.'

I'd heard this kind of thing. Sometimes pearls suddenly vanish from a river, then just as abruptly become plentiful, one mussel in every four. A pearl epidemic. Deamer had bought the estate when the owner died, and had a ready-made source of pearls for faking antique jewellery by the ton. I should have realized when Tom said that Deamer let the woods rot, yet guarded the river with obsessional fury. So whatever Deamer wanted had to be in the river. I'm thick.

'Local pearls used to be little funny-shaped things, until they came plentiful. Now they're marble-big. Some bigger, even.'

Christ. No wonder. Worth anybody's murder, almost. Guiltily I cancelled the thought. Deamer had a real winner here. Enough fantasy-baroque pearls to copy practically every famous historical brooch and pendant known.

'The river must have had an outbreak of a parasite that stimulates the mussels to make whoppers. Any fancies?' Fancies are unusual colours, deep golds to greens to purples to blacks. But be careful. Absolutely jet black pearls are difficult to sell. It's the nearly blacks—brown-blacks, greenish-blacks and blue-blacks that bring in the collectors and jewellers like wasps to fruit.

'Only now and then,' Tom said.

'Lovejoy. What *has* Deamer to do with you?' Vanessa's voice was quiet. Tom glanced back up the track where a car's lights were jolting towards us. 'Were the pearls so important that you'd send Tinker poaching them while you went to burgle Mr Deamer's house?'

'Oh, aye.' I said. No good explaining to women. 'I'm to blame sure enough.'

The car stopped. Doors slammed. Torches flashed. Somebody said, 'This where they pulled him ashore?' and a servile at-attention voice fawned, 'Yes, sir.'

Another man was saying, 'I couldn't avoid him, Ledger. The river hereabouts is so narrow.'

'So it is, sir.' Ledger's voice, all assurance. They paused then, because they were upon us.

'Wotcher, Ledger,' I said, friendly to break the ice.

'Lovejoy? What're you doing here?'

'You're a duck-egg, Ledger,' I said. 'This the gentleman that creased Tinker?'

'Accidental, Lovejoy,' Ledger said. 'We have an independent witness. A gamekeeper from Mr Deamer's estate.'

'Oh, aye.' I looked at the pale-haired man beside Ledger. 'Chatto, I presume?'

Good old Ken Chatto was taller than I remembered, and happier than a murderer has a right to be. But then he'd won the fair lady and the fortune. He and his avaricious old partner Deamer could now turn out fakes till Doomsday and be in the clear.

'Never forget a face, Kenneth.' I ignored the outstretched hand. 'What were you doing dashing upriver so fast?'

'It's a tenancy rule,' Chatto said. 'I must assist in patrolling the river with the employed gamekeepers.'

Ledger had marched to the end of the jetty and stared at the water for clues. He came back, nodding. 'Nothing here for us,' he announced. 'Show me the boat you brought Dill in with, Tom. And you, miss.'

'Will you be all right, Lovejoy?' Vanessa asked me. Chatto had made no move, and the bobby was following Tom and Ledger.

'Yes, ta. I'll shout if Kenneth annoys me.'

We watched her follow them, me sitting on the jetty and the murdering woman-stealing bastard standing beside me smiling in the gloaming.

'Well, Kenneth,' I said finally. My tea'd gone cold in all this. 'Pity about Owd Maggie and Vernon, eh?'

'It was, rather.' I stared up at him. He actually sounded sincerely sorry. 'You see, Lovejoy, Maggie'd received a spirit message. Donna overheard you phoning. There was no other way.'

So he was the nut. 'Tut-tut,' I said. 'Forced into it, eh?'

'I'm glad you understand.' He sighed, all the cares of the world. 'And I never did get on with Sidney. Especially when Donna chose between us. Did you know we were at school together? He was quite sound as a youngster, victor ludorum and all that. But spineless in later years. He lost his nerve over the old woman. Positively weak.' He sounded merely mildly put out, an elderly vicar when tea's late.

'And you did him in, so they'd arrest me?'

'Why, certainly. I had to. Mr Deamer has every right to expect reliable service. You can see that, Lovejoy.' He sounded so bloody earnest.

'I can see you're off your frigging nut.'

'How dare you!' He quivered like a pointer dog. For a second I thought he was going to boot me into the water. 'How dare you! You . . . tramp! You've lost, Lovejoy. Don't you understand? We're already spreading the word, saying your motive for killing Sidney was the pendant. Once the trade hears that, everybody will believe our products are genuine. Then we can sell fakes as genuine a hundred times over—all in under compulsory secrecy, to dealers and collectors from all over the world. It's beautiful. It can't fail, Lovejoy. Thanks to you.'

'I'd approve,' I said, 'if it weren't for Owd Maggie, Sid, me nearly getting topped. And Tinker.'

'You, Lovejoy,' said this upper-crust example of gentlemanly enterprise, 'are simply envious of my success.'

My baffled silence was still matching his affronted petulance when Ledger led the others across to say polite goodbyes. Ledger told me to make sure to report in at the police station in the morning.

'Aye, aye,' I said irritably. 'Oh, Kenneth.'

'Yes, Lovejoy?' He paused, still annoyed at me for not admiring his murderous cleverness.

'I spoke to Owd Maggie today. You've not won at all.'

Chatto recoiled and actually moaned as he turned and blundered away. Ledger glanced, followed. I lifted a hand for Tom to pull me to my feet.

'Look,' I said, as they drove off. 'I know I'm a pest, but is there any chance of a pint and a pasty? I've something on my mind.'

There was a big auction not far off. Maybe there was something we could put in . . .

'Lovely. Between one-and-a-half and three grains in weight.'

Tom was reminiscing and fugging the warm sleepy kitchen with his pipe. Vanessa was listening. Billy was sleeping upright on her lap, sometimes leaping into wakefulness with a startled murmur. I'd got the old bloke talking about his gamekeeping days as soon as we'd started on Vanessa's meat-and-potato, concentrating loosely on the local pearls of course. Natural pearls are measured by weight, four grains equals one carat. It's only cultured pearls that are measured in millimetres, because their centre is a solid mother-of-pearl bead made from a Mississippi River Valley clam.

'Oh, some whoppers,' Tom went on. 'I've seen a perfect sphere brought out when I was a lad. Size of a sparrow's egg. My grand-uncle was a poacher,' Tom explained disarmingly. 'It was his pal culled it. Forty-one grains. He bought his house with that, Lowestoft way.'

'You'll not see them often, eh?' Pearl size is all-important. Not surprising, really. It takes a poor old mollusc three years to thicken a pearl's coat a single millimetre.

'Not likely. Twisted and bent. Fishbones. When I was gamekeeping there used to be six poachers, as secret as hell. Tinker's uncle was one, the bugger. They pass it down in families.' Served me right for being too besotted with Donna to even talk with Tinker. Tom went on, 'Since Deamer took the estate and fetched in his gamekeepers we've had two poachers go.'

'Go?' I said blankly.

'Die. Accidental deaths. One drunk-drownded.' He said drown-dead like they do round here. 'One just lost. All open, like.'

'Of course.' And it would be all open, like. Deamer would plan that, and Kenneth would excecute it. An enormous depression settled on me. All along they'd proved themselves pros. No wonder Deamer thought I'd the brains of a ticket-collector. Even Donna's tempestuous love-making had been planned. Anything, including murders, to protect their wonderful pearlmine.

'February's best,' Bill was saying. 'Winter frost kills the

weeds, see? Makes the mussels easier to find. But our on-shore wind stirs up the silt.'

'Saves a few innocent mussels, though.'

Tom grinned. 'For an antique dealer you're too soft-hearted, Lovejoy.'

'For a gamekeeper you know too much about poaching.'

He was serious again. 'Only way to beat them. After all, you're not allowed to . . .' He broke off, fiddled with his pipe.

'No,' I agreed bitterly. 'You're not allowed to eliminate people who misbehave. Only Deamer and Chatto are allowed to do that.' I cheered up as one original thought blundered into my empty skull.

'Penny for them, Lovejoy?' Vanessa asked over little Billy's head.

'Just thinking, love. I've been stupid. You know why? Because I went out of my natural element. Oh, sure, sure. You were great, getting me to Deamer's house. But this desperate stuff's not my scene. What happened to Tinker and Sid Vernon and Owd Maggie proved that.'

'What is your natural element, Lovejoy?'

'Antiques, love.' I hitched my chair closer to the table for my elbows' sake. 'Any more tea?' I asked, and began, 'Listen. Once upon a time a lady hired this antique dealer and took him to a seance . . .'

And my mind was working it out: a few weeks to the big auction at Montwell. It had to be then.

CHAPTER 22

Seduction's not my greatest skill. Women are always there before me, though I try. The few times I've actually set out to make a deliberate ploy have been either abject failures—with the bird rolling in the aisles laughing and me narked as hell—or so astonishingly successful that you begin to wonder who's seducing whom. I remember one lovely bird, a woman with a wonderful dress sense and a brass Culpeper microscope, Burke and Jones of Bristol about 1780, the best. She had, one of those porcelain faces and transparent skin. I sweated blood over her, spent a fortune on talcum powder and a new razor blade. When we'd finally made smiles she said to me along the pillow, 'You know, Lovejoy, this is so overdue I was worrying what was wrong with me.' See what I mean about them being there first? Makes you wonder what women really think about all day long. Different minds from normal, I suppose.

But sometimes seduction's thrust upon you. So I came in from the rain like a drowned rat and stood dripping on the posh rugs strewn about the receptionist's office of Tierney's Auction Rooms Ltd, in Montwell. Auctioneers are the easiest of all known 'marks' for the con trick, being natural crooks themselves and therefore unable to believe it'll ever happen to them.

'Hello,' I said, beaming and making sure the inner office door was closed.

'Good morning, sir. May I help you?' The woman did the eye trick, an up-and-down glance full of scorn. To women grotty means poor, and they hate poverty with fervour, wealth being their religion.

'Yes, please,' I said, deciding to be wealthy. I never have a plan. Spontaneity works best. 'This is where the famous jewellery sales are?'

'Certainly.' She didn't quite melt, but her kilojoule of gratification was a giant step for mankind.

I shook my plastic mac to irritate. Our relationship couldn't flower without tolerance. The sooner she learned some, the better. 'I've been sent to inquire into your firm's auction practice,' I said.

'Into our firm's . . .?' She was furious.

'By Lord Eskott. I'm his confidential secretary. James, ah, Chandler.' She paused. 'A private source may send an antique item in, you see.' I hesitated to indicate a faint distaste for commerce.

'I see.' Her mind logged: a peer of the realm, death duties, a fantastically valuable heirloom, shame at things coming to such a pretty pass. Her hand moved towards one of those button telephones that never work. 'I'd better contact Mr Tierney . . .'

'Ah, no. Confidential, you see.' Snootily I looked about. 'I'm first required to make an informal assessment. You do understand?'

'Yes, yes,' she said, now a little anxious.

I pressed on quickly. 'Outside the normal channels. It's somewhat sensitive.'

'Mr Tierney usually takes, ah, significant visitors into his office.'

'Then we'll have to meet elsewhere,' I decided, facing up to duty. 'After work, possibly?'

Loyalty and propriety battled for her soul. Neither won, with her being female. Curiosity and the faintest hint of sin carried the day.

'Only to discuss confidentiality for specially valuable items,' she affirmed carefully. There was to be no funny business.

I looked her straight in the eye and smiled with utmost sincerity. 'What else?'

My apologies to Lord Stanhope Eskott, if there's a real one, because I told Olivia things about the noble Eskotts that I honestly shouldn't have mentioned to a living soul. Of course I did the decent thing, made her promise not to breathe a word and all that, but as I warmed to my task over a dainty tea in Montwell's dainty tearooms I'm afraid that quite a few scandalous disclosures tripped lightly from my tongue. Lord Eskott's daughter Felicity was a slut, son

Fanshawe a renegade, and as for Her Ladyship and that cowherd . . .

She was fascinated. Not of course by the happy bits. The tragedies and scandals went over really great.

'You mean Leandra *ran away*?' She was out of breath, her cheeks red spots, and spoon absently stirring her empty cup and driving me mad.

'Look, Olivia.' I was all stern. 'It isn't for us to judge.' The reproof established me as a pillar of rectitude.

'Why, of course not,' Olivia cried softly. 'We can't, shouldn't . . .'

But we did. We agonized over young Bertie's commission in the Household Cavalry now he'd met that actress: was she worth the risk? We were outraged by Cousin Maltravers's behaviour, going off like that. We prayed that Clara wouldn't turn out as all her mother's side had done. Those Cornish Penhaligons had bad blood.

'One thing after another,' I sighed. 'You can appreciate my difficulty.'

'Oh yes!' she breathed. 'The scandal if word got out! But Tierney's confidentiality . . .'

I put in anxiously, 'But are the personnel reliable?'

'Ah.' Olivia wagged a finger. 'I can see you don't understand how trustworthy auctioneers operate.'

'No indeed,' I said truthfully. Does anyone?

'I'll go over it right from the beginning . . .'

That was on Monday of the week after my non-raid on Deamer's house. Five weeks till the big Montwell auction. I began experimenting the very first night back in my own dowdy cottage.

Once I get going I'm quite lost in intensity. Creative art is all very well, but successful forgery has to be executed with skill, like all murders.

Love creates art; precision makes fakes.

CHAPTER 23

Work's not all beer and skittles.

What I said about art and forgery is true, yet these pinnacles of human endeavour do have common ingredients. The most important is enthusiasm, plus I'm a great believer in impetus.

One trouble was Tinker. He was really narking me. The surly old burke was living the life of Riley in hospital, chatting up the nurses and grousing whenever I called to see him. He wanted to stay abed, when I now desperately needed his help. After all, I'd almost saved his life—well, nearly almost, because it was Tom's return that stopped Chatto having another go, but I'd meant well.

Lydia was another pest, and Sandy and Mel fourteen more each at least. I kept being hauled from my workshop to referee arguments on percentages and pricing the antiques from my sweep. Mel had managed another few items as they'd gone along, the prize being a beautiful Fuller's measurer. This rarity—think of rolling-pin-sized ivory cylinders covered in ruled lines and numbers—was a unique calculating device in its day, and now costs the earth. And so it should, because nowadays we've only got grotty computers.

Between these rows I did trial after trial until the workshed's floor was littered with discarded Siren-shaped test pieces, dashed into town to see Tinker, hurtled to our pathetic library to be told there was no demand for the books I demanded, and between times got on with seducing Olivia from her tenacious loyalty at Montwell. I was knackered. Well, even Don Juan had off-days.

Still I ploughed on with instinct my sole guide, desperately worried about time.

Seven trials was my minimum, seven pieces of jewellery whose central piece was a huge baroque 'pearl', Italian Renaissance style. Six could be honestly duff, but one had to be perfect, as near the original pendant as dammit.

Two vital points about money.

The law says 'forgery' only has to do with coinage and documents. Much it knows. Legally, however, anybody can make a 'reproduction', so you can safely copy the Mona Lisa (for purely artistic reasons, of course). But 'forgery' and 'counterfeiting' and 'fake' the world over mean you intend to deceive, you rascal, you. And it's no good claiming that only King John's signature is phoney on that beautiful Magna Carta you've just made, that the rest of it is genuine parchment, ink, etc. Worse, the judges play hell even when there is no original, like if you forge your Uncle Basil's will and never had an Uncle Basil. Some counties in Scotland aren't quite so bad. For weird historical reasons they let you forge what you like, as long as you don't actually profit from it. The rest of our scatterbrained Kingdom's laws cheerfully convict you twice: once for the forgery and again for passing it. See the risk? A harsh old world.

Luckily, most antiques aren't documents. So you can make and even wear reproductions of the Crown Jewels, for all the police care. But carrying those same repros in a sack at midnight makes the peelers suspect you're going to swap the originals. Then you're for it. Intent to deceive, you see?

The other vital point is that *everything* can be copied, faked, forged, reproduced, and counterfeited. Sometimes it's respectable, like that famous ex-Presidential candidate who recently made a bomb from fakes in the US, legitimately of course. Respectability's an elastic little word. The trouble is that blokes like me, already under police surveillance, shouldn't even dream of doing anything risky. So it would have to be the path of righteousness. Worse, it would also have to be very, very legal.

Now, hand on my heart, I wasn't going to deceive a single soul and that's the honest truth. Except Lydia, and Olivia. And maybe Mel and Sandy, Deamer, Chatto, Donna, and a few score antique dealers. But you can't count any of these, because they're in the trade, and that's normal.

'Sandy,' I said carefully one morning when they arrived to do the bookwork. 'I want you to go to the harbour and with all possible secrecy bring me ten stone of herring. Soon as you can.'

He fainted a bit and screeched, then got the giggles. 'But, Lovejoy! People will stare!' And him in a feather boa and Cavalier hat. Mel would have nothing to do with it. Typically, neither asked what I wanted them for.

I'd no idea how much a stone of fish actually was, but it sounds a lot. I tried working out the ancient measure: fourteen pounds to a stone, say two herrings to a pound . . . hopeless.

'If our lovely fringes go stinky-poos, Lovejoy . . .' Sandy threatened, still tittering. 'Not Brightlingsea?'

'Not necessarily from Brightlingsea, no.'

Once Sandy'd had a tame beetle called Francisco. On a black day in Brightlingsea an itinerant picture-dealer had accidentally stood on Francisco. Sandy'd made local headlines petitioning the town council for a day of mourning. The council refused. Sandy still raises opposition to the mayor every polling day. I shrugged and went round the side of the cottage to my workshed. It's only a battered old garage, but it's where I do all my forgeries—I mean my restoration work.

The first step to forging a pearl is making the pearl's shape. Easy for 'classical' spherical pearls, but difficult for baroques. Go in two stages. First, make the 'bead', as pearl fakers call it. Traditionally this was a simple drop of glass. Nowadays clever sinners use epoxy resins and plastics because you can adjust the bead's weight (and thereby its overall relative density). Then coat your bead with pearl. A mollusc does it for nothing, but has all the time in the world. It would have to be *essence d'orient*.

Cultured pearls are often dyed; a cotton strand dipped in hydrochloric acid shows the dye when you touch a cultured pearl with it. The best way to detect artificial pearls, on the other hand, is by pressing them to your sensitive upper lip—cold means real, warmish means imitation. Spain perfected the manufacture, hence the nickname for artificial pearls, majjies, from that island's old name, Majorica. Two vital don'ts: women's magazines are forever preaching the pin test—imitation pearls show the pinprick—and (something equally daft) drying pearls with a hot-air hairdrier when you wash them. The best ways of ruining your pearl necklaces anybody could imagine.

The Siren was easy to shape in plasticine. The surface needed to be flawless. Naturally I'd got photographs of the genuine piece, from the 1971 sale when Sotheby's sold the original.

In faking antiques, shapes are simple. For speed, I settled for the faker's friend. Silicone rubber sets swiftly, doesn't need heat or separating chemicals, gives terrific detail.

While it was setting round my Siren-shaped lump of plasticine I strolled across the side lane to Kate and arranged for her to come and help me with all those bloody fish. She's one of those gnarled old coast women who know how to do things.

'Scrape herring?' she said. She was washing in a dolly-tub with a wood posser that had been used so much it was bleached, skeletal and furry.

'I want their scales. Ten stone, Kate.'

'God save us! You're a rum un, Lovejoy, no mistake.' She fell about laughing and making jokes about feeding the five thousand and all that while I waited patiently. She's really hilarious, silly old crab. 'All right, son. Give me a call.'

She sent me off with an Eccles cake, still cackling. But I was smiling too. I'd have my own pearl essence within a couple of days. Sometimes I think I'm the only person left not off my trolley. Still, life's all go when you're doing good, isn't it?

Gold, gold chain, a diamond or two, a ruby or two, a few small freshwater baroque pearls, and I was in business. I'd need help, of course, of a very special kind from very special sources, namely: Vanessa's dad (little freshwater pearls), Olivia (the Montwell auction), Sandy (fish), Kate (fish), and gold. Better not forget that.

Olivia's what folk call plain, but that's only an admission of their blindness. Her face radiated charm, her eyes an open blue. Her figure wasn't filmstar-shaped but even filmstars aren't that. I liked her for her honesty, probably that's all it was. Yet you have to be careful, because every woman has her own attractiveness and I had a serious job to do. I still wasn't sure exactly what. It was our third candlelight tryst.

'We're not supposed to, James,' she said seriously.

'Good heavens!' I cried into my complicated risotto thing. I'd asked to inspect Tierney's security arrangements. 'You don't think I meant when your clients' valuables were actually *in* Tierney's, did you? I wouldn't dream of such a thing.'

'I suppose . . .' she began doubtfully, then smiled. 'Perhaps after the Saturday clearing inventory. The offices and auction rooms will be quite empty.'

'Only if you're sure,' I said stoutly.

'I can trust you,' she glowed, and leant across the table eagerly. 'How is Anastasia, James?'

'Eh?'

'Did anything come of her meeting with Squire Wainwright?'

My poor old memory creaked into action. Where'd I been

up to? I'd become so confused with the mythical Lord
Eskott's saga that I'd taken to buying handfuls of lonely-
hearts romances and allocating one story to each character.
I couldn't keep track.

'Too much came of it, Olivia,' I replied sadly, hoping I'd
got the right tale. 'When Felicity called on him . . .'

So, suss out Tierney's auction place on Saturday. I was
in. My mind laboriously charted the beginning of a plan.
Not perfect, but other people have taught me to live with
imperfections. It seemed to me I'd need a massacre, and
immediately thought of Big John Sheehan. Horses for
courses.

CHAPTER 24

'The best pearl river in the whole Kingdom was the White-
cart,' Tom told me wistfully in a crowd of milling holiday-
makers. Vanessa was already out in the bay with Billy,
helping a sailboat that had got in trouble. Everybody was
dispiritingly hearty and nautical, as well as shamingly
matter-of-fact. 'Pollution's done for it.'

'I'd heard the Tay.'

'Ah, the mighty Tay. The greatest emperors in the world
used to send for them scotchers.' He paused reflectively.
'It's their special shine, see?'

'Then how do I get some small baroque pearls?' Deamer's
men would be trebly vigilant now.

Tom grinned. 'Buy them, Lovejoy.'

'Eh?' I said faintly. He'd gone off his head.

'Smallest are the commonest. Any good pearlie-man'll
sell them for a fiver. It's all the jewellers pay.'

'I need them soon, Tom. Practically now.'

He'd said he'd give me a couple of addresses.

★

Later I told Lydia to pop up to Perth and buy some small freshwater scotchers, if she'd enough money.

'But Perthshire's—' she clutched at the bedclothes, instantly thinking of blizzards '—*north of Edinburgh!*'

I drew her close. Why are women's knees always freezing? 'There's nobody else I can trust.'

'Will it be cold, Lovejoy?'

'Good heavens, no. Luckily, they're having an Indian summer. Unprecedented. To do with the Gulf Stream . . .'

She left that Saturday morning, with the address of that old Perth jewellery firm which still buys cleverly from the few remaining freshpearlers.

I emerged from the station having seen her off. There was a bulbous old motor on the forecourt looking familiar. The mechanic had a clipboard. 'You Lovejoy? Sign here.'

'What for?' I asked guardedly. Bailiffs assume disguises.

'It's your bleedin' car, mate.'

Disbelievingly I walked round it. It was my old Austin Ruby, still battered but on its legs again. I hadn't even noticed it had gone from the garden. Normally it's just there, rusting in solitude among the nettles.

'Does it go?' I asked. It usually didn't.

'Bloody nerve,' the mechanic said in annoyance. 'That bird would have had our balls. She interrupted our frigging tea-break to make sure.' He was very bitter, so I signed. 'And she only paid half the bill. The other half if it runs for a month.'

The crank-handle swung like a lamb bringing the old crate clattering to life. I climbed in—the doors don't work—unleashed the savage power of all its seven horse-power, and rattled grandly off. Things were coming up roses. I started singing a Tallis *Gaude*.

Ledger pulled me in, first set of traffic lights.

Ledger was grandly seated in his posh office, happy as a hustler. Chandler was there too, feet up on the desk.

'Don't say anything, Lovejoy. Just listen.'

My complaints died unspoken. I'm never the type to have a merry quip ready. I only think of cutting remarks on the way home.

Ledger pointed with a pencil. 'This is a warning, lad. Just three words. Don't do it.'

'Don't do what?'

Ledger sighed. 'I told you to shut up, Lovejoy.'

'He's trouble, Ledgie.' Chandler slammed his boots to the floor and rose. 'This bastard's up to something. It stinks a mile off. Look at him.'

When the Old Bill hauls you in for nothing you find reassurance in the little things of life: an old lady visible through the glass partition waiting to be seen about her missing poodle; a typist clacking away in the next office; a slit-view of the street door and people on the pavement.

'Lovejoy,' Ledger continued wearily, 'you have a grievance. Against Mrs Vernon, Deamer, Chatto. Even,' he ended, smiling hopefully, 'against the police.'

Once, in the Army, I saw a bloke viciously punished for 'dumb insolence', that most nebulous of non-criminal crimes. It frightened me badly. Like now. Chandler was taking short irritable strides around the room, breathing in time. Suddenly I didn't want Ledger to leave. I stayed dumb and still.

'He's a villain, Ledgie.' Chandler's face was blotched.

Ledger continued, 'You're now mobile, Lovejoy, with that old sewing-machine parked outside disgracing the street. So I'm warning you. For the next few weeks you're a pure little choirboy. D'you hear?'

A nod from me. Chandler was still smouldering, pacing.

'Now go. Report at the desk every morning before ten.'

I began, 'You can't make me do that—'

Chandler grabbed me. Somehow I was instantly hurtling through the air and across the corridor. I just managed to hit the wall with my shoulder to stop my skull splatting the bricks. I tumbled and crawled a yard, my head reeling. The old lady had nodded off and didn't even rouse. The typist clacked on. A uniformed bobby strolled indifferently by in barge boots.

The desk sergeant was a bloke I knew quite well. I'd played against him in a crown-green bowling match once. He did the police trick of pretending to be busy. Crime could flourish unhindered. Wincing, I wobbled upright, holding on to the wall.

'Here, Gerry,' I said conversationally. 'What did psychopaths do for a living before the police were formed?'

He avoided my eye, so I avoided his to show I'd got pride. I was thinking: Well, well. Good old Chandler in with Deamer's mob, and Ledger too thick to see it. The whole thing one composite pattern at last.

Even though the police had given me a parking ticket, my heart was singing. The road was doing my driving with a vengeance now. Time to call in the gangsters. No problem there; everybody's got a lot of those.

I'm not proud of that Saturday, though everything went superbly. All right, Olivia showed me round Tierney's after the rest of the staff had gone. And all right, I was full of good reasons like a con trick and crippling a few people, so morally I was on the firm grounds of justice and whatnot. The trouble is I find there are always unexpected consequences. They're never my fault, but life has a habit of rapping you over the knuckles even for getting things right. It's really unfair.

In the auction firm's offices Olivia showed me the jewellery trays—metal based, with a locked fenestrated Perspex cover; you can look at and touch items but not move them. They were bad news. The safe was easier, an ancient cube no self-respecting burglar would unpack his toolkit for. Then, with the dreaded tyranny of the garrulous, she decided we ought to stop off at a quiet place on the coast road, to make sure we'd forgotten nothing. We did stop, off, and did make sure. She was smooth, assured, pleased and pleasing. I won't go into details. Enough to say a bond was forged between us most of that night. I'm not grumbling. Worse things happen at sea, as they say.

Sunday dawned before I reached the cottage, done for. I was practically certain that she still didn't suspect: to her I was still James Chandler, a bona fide Tierney customer. I think. Anyway, plenty of time before evensong to set my trap and organize the fake. Illegalities are always straightforward. It's the honest bits that always need bending round odd moral corners.

I'd had an early breakfast with Olivia. Weak but hopeful, I set to work in the shed with my plan at last in place. Later, I'd phone Big John Sheehan, God help me.

Faking pearls is as old as Man's love for pearls themselves, but not by this method I was going to try: epoxy resin mixed with mucoidal goo from fish scales.

As I worked on in the slanting sunshine, I pondered other possible ways. From the Middle Ages to the nineteenth century, fakers tried wax-covered gypsum or alabaster beads soaked in oil. They sound really gungey but are surprisingly convincing when fresh. Age is the give-away here; they don't last. Or you can polish mother-of-pearl into beads—nice from a distance, but they look all little layers close to.

The French fakers' favourite method's glass beads coated with fish-scale scrapings stuck on by parchment glue with a drop of wax. The best fish-scale solution is Canadian, incidentally. It's oily stuff called guamine. Scrape fish scales into water and you see it glowing at the bottom. People ship it in vinegar or ammonia that burns your eyes. The old fakers' formulas: 20,000 bleak fish for a pound of the pearly mucus; 1,000 fake pearls from three ounces. Some use a drop of gum tragacanth. Opal-glass 'pearls' never fooled anybody, and apart from the new plastic jobs there's not

much else. You see how difficult the faking game is? Life's
a real wind-up.

Sandy telephoned at an ungodly hour the next morning.
He'd ordered the fish. ('Mel's absolutely livid! Just because
I was having a little chat-a-tête with a such pretty sailor—')

In the garden I rigged up a plastic funnel over a wine-
maker's glass carboy half-filled with water. Me and a Ches-
terfield bloke had done it once before so I knew it stank the
place out. I'd nip along the footpath, tell Kate they were
coming, then hid in the workshed till it was all over. I'm
not squeamish, but the less I saw of it the better. She
had a nephew who'd take the fish corpses off my hands.
Meanwhile it was crank the Ruby out of somnolescence and
trundle to town.

CHAPTER 25

Sitting on the floor in Herbie Belcher's garret while he fired
a dress ring's mountant, I mentally examined Tierney's
safety procedure. It sounds pretty hopeless security, but
think a minute. All small precious items locked into viewing
trays. A whizzer always stands by. The senior Tierney
alone holds the key. Lovely items such as jewels, pendants,
necklaces, rings, are only brought out under guard ten
minutes before the doors open to the rapacious public.

'A simple swap's the most difficult.'

'What, Lovejoy?'

Herbie had finished, switching off his jet burner and
raising his protective glasses. I must have spoken aloud.

'Nothing, Herbie.' I grinned innocently.

'Oh, aye,' he said distrustfully. 'What you want, Lovejoy?'

Herbie Belcher has more forgeries masquerading in famous museums than any goldsmith I've ever met. He used to

work in a Whitechapel sweatshop as a kid, rising to Hatton Garden by talent. He works in this creaking attic down the Dutch Quarter, the part of our town I told you about. Herbie's place is a pleasure to visit: a five-recessed jeweller's bench straight out of the French eighteenth century, covered in goldsmithy mini-tools. His floor's covered by caies, those wooden Joliot grills for scraping gold dust off people's boots. You wouldn't laugh if ever you see the gold dust Herbie cleans off them every Easter. Lovely to see the old geezer work. I once saw him fake a Roman fertility ring in 22-carat; out of this world. He doesn't have windows for natural daylight, simply does everything under a bare bulb.

'Seven mounts, one gold, Herbie,' I said.

'Of what?' Note: fakers never ask what for. They already know.

'This.' I passed him a piece cast like the big baroque pearl from the pendant, and my mock-up of the gold Siren mount.

He squinted at me, his metal files rippling. 'It's like that Canning Siren thing Sotheby's flogged to the Yanks.'

'Good heavens,' I said evenly. Silence.

He frowned. 'How soon? I'm up to my—'

'A fortnight, Herbie.' I rose, dusted my knees.

'Gawd almighty, Lovejoy.'

'A friend's bringing the little scotcher baroques.'

'Lovejoy,' Herbie wailed after me as I headed downstairs, 'doesn't that pendant have a diamond for a mirror? Where'll I get them?'

'Heat a few crabby old zirconites from Woolworths,' I bawled up irritably. 'Do I have to explain every bloody thing?' People really nark me. No common sense.

'It'll cost you, Lovejoy.'

His bitter refrain followed me as I opened the street door and let myself out by the ironmonger's. I didn't even bother to answer. Honestly, you try to throw money into people's pockets and what thanks do you get?

The town's one unvandalized public phone stands in a row of six by the Arcade. I went in with a heap of coins. Thugs don't make me nervous, so I was surprised to see my fingers having a clammy time finding the coin slot.

'Sheehan's,' a voice said tunelessly.

'Put John S. on,' I said, despising myself for a shake in my throat.

'Get knotted.' Click, burr.

Another trembled dialling, and the same unstructured voice said if that's the same burke calling again he'd personally crawl down the wire and spread me.

'Listen, creep,' I quavered. 'Keep John S. away from Montwell.'

Duty done, I slammed the receiver and nervously wiped my hands. Big John Sheehan is a wild Ulsterman who occasionally holidays from his devotions to play North London's antique trade. He's a 'roller', as we call them. Rollers are very wealthy and don't give a damn about antiques—as long as they're genuine. Paul Getty was one. Big John Sheehan is another, and has an army of bad lads who offer to prove it when required. His smoking cheque-book causes riots even in hallowed Bond Street. He was sure to have heard of Tierney's forthcoming auction, because he has a dolly-bird just for cataloguing catalogues. Nothing now would stop him burning up the A12 on auction day. Nobody warns John S. off.

Full of pride at a job well done, I took Margaret Dainty to the Three Cups. She was really pleased and, holding my hand, agreed to sell me an intact William Spooner antique jigsaw 'The Sugar Plantation' for less than its value. Of course I had to pay her by an IOU, but that's what IOUs are for, isn't it?

All I wanted now was to hear word that Deamer would be sending his most valuable fake into Tierney's auction, because we have a tame cracksman working locally called Fingers. He can open elderly Chubbs without splitting a fingernail. The night before the auction I'd simply get Fingers to swap Deamer's fake Siren for mine. And why? Because the baroque pearl in mine would be fake, and Donna's mob's piece had a genuine one, of the huge sort denied me. Big-spending John Sheehan would be there on auction day and buy my fake Siren—and then go after Deamer, Chatto and Donna Vernon to express his sincerest disappointment. And I'd be in the clear.

With, of course, Deamer's very, very pricey fake in my grasp. Nothing could go wrong—once Deamer lodged his item in Tierney's auction.

No news the first week, but so what? Plenty of time. Five weeks is five weeks, after all. That Tuesday I waited on the bypass, soaked to the skin, at half-three one rainy morning, for a certain long-distance haulage wagon, our nation's best and cheapest antiques delivery service. And collected two tiny leather bags of freshwater baroques from Perth, lovely little things that had cost Lydia an arm and a leg but which delighted Herbie Belcher so much that he actually smiled. She arrived safely that Wednesday, bringing a bag of Birmingham scrap mother-of-pearl, clever girl. The rest of the week was wasted in joyous reunion, so was uneventful.

No news the second week. Fine, though. Four weeks is four weeks. Long time, no? By then I had pressed imprints of Tierney's office key. I cut the key myself from sheet brass, taking great care.

My faked massive baroque pearl was finished. A couple of the trial pieces even looked great. The rest were manky. Before I let Herbie have the best I would give it one last coat, then touch it up on Finger's big night.

Three weeks gone. Still no news of Deamer's sending his pendant into Tierney's auction. But why worry?

Tierney's had type-set the sale catalogues. Olivia let me

see the proofs. I booked Fingers to do the swap, sixty quid down and a percentage.

Thursday of that week I had a blazing row with Mel, who'd taken the lid off a silver wax-jack. It's a cylindrical cup-like thing with a waxy taper uncoiling through the conical lid. 'Ignorant bloody fools like you give idiocy a bad name,' I yelled at him. How I didn't hit him I'll never know. 'Just to stretch the lid into a small dish? You frigging nerk. Any goon can detect a stretcher case.' Especially when the silversmith's mark is the famous tall rectangle of the Hennells, 1802. Sandy frantically tried to calm me but I told him to get that ugly daubed scrapheap of a car out of my bloody way, and drove off, leaving him sobbing and Mel with one of his heads.

All in all, the usual scene of Lovejoy waiting patiently.

Fourth week. No news. I was broke, on edge. Tierney's had sent out the sale catalogues. I couldn't concentrate. Tinker moaned that we were missing bargains right, left and centre. I owed everybody for everything.

Friday night I walked past a genuine Valenciennes lace sampler—you wear out two sets of eyes to make those lace edgings. Only a yard long and not two inches wide, but skilled lacemakers did one inch slogging non-stop 4 a.m. to dusk.

Saturday I stared unseeing in the Arcade while Vera Spelman and her new bloke Trevor bought a collection of six Victorian miniature baptismal fonts, replicas in stone copied from Lincolnshire churches, the sort collectors search a lifetime for. I tell you I was really on form.

Herbie Belcher finished the last of the mounts, a lovely job. The best was brilliant.

Fifth week. A week to go. And no news from Olivia. I was seeing her nightly now, ratty as hell, still pretending I was somebody called James Chandler but with my stories about

Lord Eskott's dippy family more confused than ever. And she was wearing me out. They now expected us as a routine at her bloody motel. Lydia was becoming suspicious. East Anglia was agog about the forthcoming auction at Montwell. Tierney's had taken massive double spread adverts locally and quarter boxes in the London dailies. Syndicates were forming, breaking, re-coalescing. All known antique dealers were everywhere, up to everything.

Word came of two London mobs preparing to lam in on auction day. The Cambridge dealers were already arriving. The Brixton and Southend mobs were in the two major hotels, snooker and gin till all hours. The Norwich dealers would arrive on the day, their sly habit. Rumour spread wider, faster. A Birmingham ring's lawyer was seen lunching with the senior Tierney. Big John Sheehan was coming. Christ. I couldn't sleep. When I wasn't with Olivia I was in my workshed checking and rechecking my fake pendant.

Herbie Belcher presented me with his bill. I nearly infarcted. Great. I'd now ruined myself, having had seven fakes made for nothing.

Two days left. No news but multo rumour.

Debts everywhere, and a pocketful of fakes. Big John S. was lodged in Colchester, ready for the grand drive to Montwell on the day. His Rolls puddle-splashed me by the war memorial. Lydia gave me a stern lecture on morality. Olivia lectured me mistily on togetherness. I'd have given anything for a kip.

One day left. I was done for. Display day, when all items go on show. Fingers, my cracksman swap-merchant, was drinking at the George, poised.

Disconsolately I drove over to Montwell on my own and just about made the hundred-yard walk to Tierney's auction rooms. I'd never felt so washed out. It was the usual sordid scene, antiques crammed higgledy-piggledy into the aroma of must, age and cheap new wood. Normally I'd be thrilled at the turmoil. Today it was a throng about my scaffold.

The main display cabinet was surrounded by a mass of dealers, Big John Sheehan's red head showing tallest. I sat wearily on a small oak monk's chest, depressed and exhausted by the whole thing. Olivia was at her desk listing postal bidders. She tried to give me a secret loving smile but I was too done and pretended not to see.

Then Ledger, bless him, made my day. Never say our policemen aren't wonderful, because this angel was suddenly beside me.

'Outside, Lovejoy,' he said.

'What for now, Ledger?' I didn't move. I was too tired from losing. Usually only women make me feel like this.

'Because I said, that's what for.'

I looked towards the crowd of dealers. Then I looked up at Ledger. This important peeler had made a special trip to Montwell to warn me off. A faint glow began to spread through me. My memory searched and doubtfully diagnosed the glow as optimism, the stuff I once felt every single day. Would Ledger go to all that trouble, unless . . .?

'Can't I have just one look at it, Ledgie?' I cringed.

'No,' he said. 'Up. Out.'

My spirits rose. I'd said 'it'. He knew I meant Deamer's fake, the Siren ringer. *It was here.*

'Very well,' I said, smiling beatifically and heading for the street. I walked for the sake of appearances but I could have flown.

Suspicious at my good humour, he stood watching at the exit. 'Lovejoy, you don't come near this place. Hear me?'

'I promise, Ledgie,' I told him. My heart was singing, because my scam was on. 'Oh, will you pass Chandler a message, please? Tell him no hard feelings.'

That ended his satisfaction. I went off whistling the difficult bit in Purcell's *Rejoice,* the slow rising crescendo bit that everybody in our choir gets wrong except me.

★

That same night I was in paradise. My forgery was beautiful. Old Herbie deserved a peerage, and my fake baroque pearl which formed the mermaid's torso would fool anybody—at first. The small dangling baroque pearls were Lydia's genuine scotchers, so no worry there. The gold chains and the Siren's body were Herbie's gold. Herbie had copied the mediæval Italian goldsmith's VD mark with loving care. The whole piece dazzled. The other six were marred by slight defects here and there, which was only to be expected for trials. Once the scam was over I'd sell them to some bone-headed roving dealers as they passed through.

Those small cardboard boxes that they sell digital watches in are the only really useful things you can buy from watchmakers nowadays. I'd had a nice one ready some time. Covered in imitation blue velvet, these cost about fivepence, wholesale. I'd lined it with felt over recessed polystyrene to hold the pendant tight but not rigid. Finally the whole lot was wrapped in a piece of black slub silk for ease of handling during the dark hours. I left the rest of the pendants in a safe floor-hole.

Fingers would need cash for tonight's work. Early that evening I drove to Dragonsdale and offered to sell Liz Sandwell two precious antiques I hadn't got.

'Tomorrow's jewellery auction at Montwell?' she guessed, smiling. She's a luscious bird, but her bloke's one of these rugby maniacs the size of our church. She also has that special woman's smile which eggs a man to try it on. 'The whole world'll be competing.'

'Mind your own business, wench,' I rebuked. 'I've a coconut chalice made in a debtors' prison, 1830, bone-rimmed and inlaid, with a coconut ladle. That's one.' She gasped gratifyingly, knowing the rarity of these Dickensian artefacts. 'And I've a Queen Anne period kitchen spoon rack, eighteen inches tall.'

'What about—?'

'My fingerstocks?' She'd only been about to ask if I'd any spoons to go with the rack, but I chose to misunderstand. 'You heard of them, eh? Those children's fingerstocks are all I'd have left, Liz.'

Our dear great-grandparents must have been hellraisers as infants. Their Victorian schoolteachers carved flat wood into bean-shaped pieces, each four-inch crescent with four holes and a thong. You used the leather thongs to tie troublesome pupils' hands, fingers rammed into the holes, thereby creating more disturbed personalities to educate the next generation. I knew Liz was specially interested in infant welfare. 'No deal, Liz. I'll give them as a christening present for your first.'

We bantered lightly over prices. I got a good deposit out of her for all three, fingerstocks included, and a guarantee of the balance payable at the Swan in Montwell immediately Tierney's auction was over. I said my thanks and drove off. God knows where I'd find antiques that rare, but that was tomorrow's problem. Maybe Sandy and Mel would help. Finding such genuine rarities was a long shot. I'd only ever seen one set of children's fingerstocks, in York years ago.

Lydia arrived sevenish. One look at her face and I knew something was wrong. I'd sent her negotiating all day for some tallow-candle maker's equipment, mid-Regency, from those Bury rogues.

'What is it, sunshine?'

Her gaze was on me, her eyes brimming with sorrow. She said, 'Oh, Lovejoy,' in that hopeless voice I really don't like. 'I had to come through Montwell.'

'So?'

'I saw Chandler in a restaurant with Mr Tierney's secretary.' I said nothing. She went on, 'The one you've been seeing so much of lately, Lovejoy.'

'Look. I can explain—'

'And can you explain why already there are policemen patrolling Tierney's auction yard?'

'Here,' I said with sudden indignation. 'You don't come through Montwell from St Edmundsbury.'

'All right, Lovejoy. I admit I was checking.'

See what I mean about women and slyth? But it was really disturbing. I began questioning her, chapter and verse, and finished up telling all—well, nearly all.

She heard me out.

'So when Mr Sheehan had it rated for insurance,' she reasoned, 'he would blame Mr Deamer?'

'Mmmmh,' I said, thoughtless in my gloom.

She said quietly, 'Because Mr Sheehan is prominently antisocial, Lovejoy?'

Too late I saw my mistake. 'You surely don't think—'

Her hand was held out imperiously. 'That pendant, Lovejoy.'

She undid the box and lifted the pendant against the light. I tried dissuading but it's hopeless when she's like this. It took her two minutes of silent concentration with a hand lens before she spotted it. Her face was white. Hands on her lap, she observed me with eyes like stone.

'Lovejoy. You've made a deliberate mistake.'

I was amazed. 'Me? Are you sure? Let's see—'

'You've deliberately hatched part of the epoxy base's underlayer, to show that the pearl's fraudulent.' She wouldn't give it me. 'Lovejoy. Do you know what would happen? Mr Sheehan would have purchased your forgery, and wreaked vengeance on Mr Deamer, Mr Chatto and Mrs Vernon.' Sounded all right to me, but her eyes were brimming with tears. 'Oh, Lovejoy. How could you want such a—?'

'Honestly.' I was up and pacing agitatedly. 'The things you say. Do you suppose for one minute that—'

'Well, it shan't happen.' She rose with that poisonous purity women know and love.

My vision darkened. I'd slogged bloody weeks, bank-rupted myself and alienated a galaxy. 'Oh no?'

'Your evil designs will avail you nothing,' she said straight out of a Corelli passion-rouser. Then she chucked the pendant into the fire.

CHAPTER 26

Dying embers crinkle. While I watched from the rug the fireglow faded from red to black, then black to grey powder, tiny gunshots and distant tingling cymbals sounding. The grate was an entire world. Miniature avalanches of white ash trembled, fell. Coke caverns tumbled and spat. Looking into cinders is a prelude to madness. Put as harshly as Lydia said, all right I admit it sounded pretty gothic and immoral. But what's to be done when morality is helpless, and evil rides the land? I honestly do wish that sometimes women would make allowance for purity of conviction in a man, but they never do. It's a weakness that makes me question their basic honesty.

All finished now. Fingers would watch the pub clock, and go home. Deamer and Chatto would make a fortune by selling their replicas as genuine. It might never get detected, unless another divvie chanced upon it. And they could claim that Lovejoy the divvie had once been charged with murder while trying to possess it. No better authentication among dealers.

Everything in antiques is time. That's why this game's so much like life itself, because all life is time. Normally I'm basically kind and unselfish. Everybody knows. I should have absorbed this disappointment with little more than a shrug. Not her fault of course that Lydia had so little sense, being a bird and therefore unable to see the main issues with my transparent clarity. But forgiving her didn't help the scam, which was now extinguished like the fire ash. I'd lost.

The misshapen gold mass was on the tile fender, long since cold. I'd got it out with the tongs from the fire tiger. The pearls were gone, the tiny genuine scotch baroques and my lovely fake massive one. Herbie's lovely goldwork was heat-mangled and scratched. Part of one of the little chains was missing. *Sic transit gloria mundi.* Tomorrow the auction would run its course. Deamer's forgery would be successfully auctioned. Whatever ensued, Deamer could always claim he'd submitted an authentic antique, and that any skulduggery must have occurred subsequently. God knows, I thought bitterly, it's happened often enough. Scams these days can be pulled even safer after an auction, when you think of the precautions auctioneers take beforehand. Back in the evil old days, when shops smelled of what they sold and grocers weighed tea and before gramophones turned into disceroonis, people used to smile hello even to strangers on lonely streets. Remember? Now, you're lucky to walk by unscathed. Hoping for a smile's like begging a limb. Look what social advance has done to us all.

Ashes settled with a crackle, making me jump. What was it that I had just thought? Scams these days can be pulled even safer, *even safer after an auction* . . .

But Lydia had ruined my beautiful forgery. I now had nothing to pull a scam with. Doubtless Ledger's peelers were now lurking around Tierney's auction rooms and hungry for promotion. Montwell was ticker-taped in warrant cards waiting for me to show. My six trial pieces were hopeless. The best would take a week at least to make perfect. No: but Olivia was evidently in police confidence, so Chandler was expecting me to show. *Chandler had known I was coming*—and in spite of Ledger's warning.

It was a trap, all for little me. But why would one peeler, Ledger, warn me off and another peeler, Chandler, bait the trap? Because Chandler was a rotten apple in the local constabulary, that's why.

Thinking, I actually felt myself coming out of my gloom. Since when have law, morality, police and propriety ever got in the way of honest living? Quietly I rose and stretched.

Lydia was asleep, or pretending, so I wrote a message:

Lydia,

Immediately get hold of Michaela French, Lincoln. Talk a genuine antique Jewish marriage ring off her. Fetch it by a night lorry before morning. Enter the ring into Tierney's auction by ten o'clock, and be carrying my marker loupe.

I forgive you for that horrible behaviour. Moral upbringing isn't anybody's fault. Please.

Lovejoy

Then I set the alarm clock for two-thirty, one hour's time, and put it on the table with the note.

Somehow in the scanty hours between dawn and high noon, I would sacrifice myself to Big John's merry band and so punish morality for daring to lay down rules for us righteous folk.

It was a long bicycle trek. Two trudged detours across farmland, one at least a mile, including a nasty encounter with a fool of a sheepdog with ideas of grandeur. A fitful kip in St Olave's church in Montwell until the rain-soaked wind blew the night off the country. A cat miaowed in the street outside. A milk float rattled. A postman called a greeting to somebody.

Dawn.

I left the bicycle as a temporary loan in the vestry, and cleaned myself up in the baptismal font. Pity babies don't shave or I'd have borrowed their razor.

CHAPTER 27

There's always a well-worn pub and sleazy nosh bar within spitting distance of an auction, as part of our basic training. I should be used to them by now, but it was agony, peering longingly towards the auction rooms from the pub's nooky porch. The luscious antiques called to me with their sweet mystic chime and I couldn't even cross the road. I was heartbroken. Man doth live on bread alone, if antiques are thrown in as well.

Five minutes to go. I dialled from Montwell's post office, feeling a nerk from having to doorway-dodge up the street of lovely tilted Elizabethan black-and-white houses. I asked for Mr Sheehan when the hotel switchboard answered. The bloke was even more threatening.

'Listen,' I said. No disguised voices now. 'Warn John to be careful at today's auction.' It took me three goes to say my name. 'Tell him Lovejoy rang.' That's done it, I thought. Sooner or later Sheehan's lads would come for me, no matter what happened now. A bobby was sauntering past so I had to wait. I nearly missed seeing Lydia. She did one of those flickering I'm-not-looking searches as she parked my old Ruby and went in with the drift of dealers and other thieves. Her arrival meant she had the ring from Lincoln, or something very like it. I hoped she was keeping track of who owed what to whom. La French hadn't exactly seemed full of charity.

At ten-thirty I nipped into the Lamb and Flag. It was almost empty. Morning's too early for drinking so I gave symbolic sips to a pint in a window alcove. Dealers were still arriving in all sorts of cars. Ten minutes and here came Big John Sheehan. I thought: Oh Jesus.

Two of his men stood with ominous patience on the

pavement. Big John descended in a fawn-tan overcoat, shoes gleaming and hair slicked down just as I remembered him. He stared about. Go in, you bastard, I urged mentally. Get in and buy the bloody thing. He took a full statuesque minute sussing out the street, the peelers, the traffic. He even stared across directly at my leaded glass. He couldn't see through, but his gaze shrank me. My mouth was dry. Some muscle quivered in my neck. Abruptly Big John decided, stepped inside. One of his goons waited outside facing the street. His Rolls-Royce wafted away.

Action.

There isn't a lot you can do when you're deprived of antiques. The worst pain in the world when gorgeous silver, antique jewellery, porcelain, and Sheraton and Hepplewhite and Chippendales are being whisked away before your very eyes by the undeserving.

Eleven o'clock. Montwell isn't much of a place, but it had mustered enough shoppers and cars for my purposes when I guessed the lot numbers must be nearing 150. Big John must have looked his fill at the jewellery by now. He'd be standing in that immobile pose I knew so well. Even expert bidders are sometimes daunted into silence when his rumbling voice begins to bid. He always calls the same, 'Here, sir.' No eyebrow-twitching theatricals from him. John Sheehan's not a bad bloke, as homicidal psychopaths go, but I wouldn't fancy being in the way when he's moving. He isn't as gigantic as all that. He actually gets his name from dealing in 'biggies', those high value one-offs which set our dark trade aglitter.

Time to go and get caught. I rose. My half-empty pint fell. I didn't even pause as the annoyed barmaid tutted. Out into the windy street. Cross between two slow cars hunting for parking space.

To the right of the auction rooms runs a wall, with the big double gate carrying the legend *J. & S. Tierney*. A fresh-faced bobby stood in front of the postern gate as if it were a Victorian fireplace.

' 'Morning. I'm due inside,' I told him.

'Not this way, sir. Through the auction-room entrance.'

'I'm in the vendors' list,' I explained, beaming. 'So I'm allowed. A last-minute lot. I have to see to the details. Late-listers never get documented up front once an auction's begun.'

The constable hesitated, pulled out a communicator and blurted crisp syllables. The postern door opened. I stepped inside with a smile and a word of thanks, and froze between two grinning constables.

' 'Morning, Lovejoy,' said Chandler. Nobody else in the yard but Tierney's security man. 'Stand still, Lovejoy. Lads, remove that forgery from his person.' Why is it that happiness makes some people repellent? The bobbies set about me.

'Forgery, Sergeant?'

'Don't play the goat, Lovejoy. Of a certain siren-design antique.' He stood there, never moving his eyes. God, he was hateful. Thank heavens they're not armed.

They were very personal and increasingly discomfited as they found nothing and more nothing.

'He's got a dirty comb and two quid, Sarge.'

'The lining, laddie.'

One bobby slit the cloth and extracted a button and a penny among fluff. Chandler was puzzled. He'd been so certain I would be carrying a fake. While Chandler's cortex tried to reactivate I said, 'If I can have my shoes back. Ta.' I said my say about a late entry, and shuffled towards the office steps. I dressed on the move with a clumsy attempt at dignity, but it's difficult with your clobber trailing.

'Lot one-sixty,' Tierney's voice squawked. They have a tannoy.

Chandler called, 'Stay with him, Perry. Woolfson, go and join Keeling. Stick by that apprentice tart of his.' The

Keystone Kops were out in force all right. Burglars all over East Anglia must be thinking it was Christmas.

'Knock, knock,' I said, smiling up the stairs to the Tierney guard. 'Late entry registered at ten o'clock. Name of Lovejoy.' The guard opened the door without a glance at it, his gaze fixed on me, memorizing like mad.

Olivia was staring as I crossed the office, an odd expression on her face. A portly whizzer stood guard by the door which opened into the crowded auction room. Constable Perry cleared his throat for a husky greeting and positioned himself to block my retreat.

'Lot one-six-one,' Tierney squeaked. Here it came. The crowd hushed. Dealers focused alcohol-shot eyes on catalogues. 'Antique Italian pearl and gold pendant, of genuine Siren pattern and by the same maker as the famous . . .' tra-la, tra-la.

'Showing here, sir!' The whizzer's traditional cry rose.

'James!' Olivia said in a strangled voice.

'Why, yes,' I said, smiling pleasantly. 'I'm a late-lister. Jewish canopied marriage ring. Under the name Lovejoy.' My admission shook her. She stared, nodded, worked on at the console. Michaela French's Jewish ring lay on the office table, with three other last-minute entries. 'Ah, there it is. Nice piece, isn't it?'

In the hall the bidding for Deamer's fake began. Lydia was hovering, now so pale she looked transparent. And Donna. And Chatto. Birds of a feather, Chandler had said. Constable Woolfson joined another peeler, pushing through the mob. They muttered together, helmets nodding, glancing into the office with meaning.

'Here, sir.' That was Big John's voice bidding. I experienced a new feeling twice as sinking, twice as fast.

'Never seen such a big crowd at an auction,' I said to Olivia. 'Don't let me interrupt.'

She was busy with the print-out, tapping the computer keys, by now completely thrown. Giving my real name had

told her I knew I'd walked into Chandler's trap. Her face
was on fire. She didn't look up at me.

A buzz from the crowd. Deamer's fake was sold. Some
fool actually clapped, a high price. The hatch crashed and
a tray came through. A tiny green point of reflection from
the console screen caught my eye.

Cameras. Four. One at each top corner of the office. All
on me. Upstairs must be like Fighter Control. Clearly this
was a police operation. They were going to get me no matter
what.

'Lot one-six-two,' the auctioneer bleated. I saw Big John
Sheehan's head turn. He'd won the bidding. One of his men
would be coming to pay.

'Here, Lyd.' I beckoned to Lydia through the doorway.
She turned in the crowd. 'Our ring that you entered. Did
you check the stone?'

She got the message. 'Er, yes. Just now.'

The door guard stepped between Lydia and me. For a
ghastly second whole wars struggled on her face. Sin battled
truth. Morality assaulted loyalty.

I looked at her. 'You sure?'

'Why, yes,' Lydia decided, fumbled in her handbag. The
two police moved to watch her. 'It's as described. Here.'

'Quiet during the bidding,' Tierney called.

I reached over the guard's shoulder and took the eye-glass
from her. Not much bigger than a thimble, and transparent.
I showed it casually to the guard on my palm, peered quickly
at the ring, 'Mmmh. I suppose it's okay . . .'

The hatch crashed open. A tray slid through on to Olivia's
desk. The hatch slammed.

'This that famous pendant?' I said, and bent for a quick
peer as Olivia exclaimed and boots clumped closer. They'd
be breathing faster upstairs, Universal Studios on audit day.

The pendant on the tray was bonny, even if it was fake.
The forgers had done a great job for Deamer. It was held
immovably under the grid. No chance of lifting it without

permission. Like touching a woman's knee through a hole in her stocking.

'Watch me, Constable,' I joked warningly. The mermaid's golden body swam into my vision as I peered at her through the eyeglass, monocle-style.

'Please don't touch,' Olivia said.

'I won't. Hold on, though.'

I murmured as if spotting something rather worrying, holding the rim of the eyeglass as if inspecting some minute flaw.

Old Denny Jackson from Clacton had showed me how to deface stuff this slick one-handed way. Actually it isn't a bad method of engraving. Once, jewellers used an engraver's needle projecting from a microscope's objective lens. Nowadays it's easier to clip the point from a record-player's stylus and Araldite it to an eyeglass. They're small enough to go unnoticed. It's not a well-known technique, and it's certainly underrated. Except for me, I've only ever seen Denny do it properly, and he's a rogue. 'No-o-o,' I said slowly, still apparently examining away. 'I'm still unsure about it.' I straightened up, pretending disappointment for the cameras' sake. 'Thanks, Lyd.' I made to pass the eyeglass and dropped it. Nine out of ten times they fall on their cylindrical sides and get picked up by their edges. The whizzer warded me off with his arms. He too was waiting for the police to close in. He stooped, passing the loupe to Lydia.

'Thank you,' Lydia said faintly, and moved off.

'About my Jewish marriage ring, Olivia. No reserve price, please.' I placed myself in front of her desk and touched her hand on the computer keyboard. 'Are you all right?'

'Of course,' she said. My apparent innocence was rattling her. I should have been arrested by now, and nothing had happened, yet still she kept up the act.

Sometimes I wonder if women aren't incapable of having friends. Maybe by nature they can only make lovers and haters. Olivia had been told everything, leading me on to have me caught. The ultimate of a lifetime, sinning to do right.

I went to the exit door where Constable Perry waited. 'Another search, or can I go, Constable?'

'Lot one-six-one, lady,' a goon was saying behind me in that cold voice I remembered from my phone calls. Big John's nerk had come to pay and collect.

Perry and the guard searched me outside on the steps, but it wasn't the breeze which made me shiver. The first thing Sheehan would do would be to get some expert to check the pendant's authenticity. Any jeweller worth his pay would find the sign scratched on it. It was my very own mark: *Ly ft: Lovejoy fecit.* Then the heads would roll, including maybe mine. But as long as they included Deamer's and Donna's and Chatto's I wouldn't mind. Much.

CHAPTER 28

Ever gone through a period when stress suddenly ends? I staggered across to the Lamb and Flag.

'I can remember,' I told the barmaid scathingly as I paid her, 'when a pint cost a groat.'

'You seen the price of groats lately?' she said. A know-all. In her job she must know more about the antiques trade than anyone on earth.

I came over all of a do and sat quivering, overlooking the road until Lydia came over. She'd collected the money we'd got from the Jewish marital ring.

'Not a bad price,' I praised, except La French would kill me for not having the gelt to pay her for it.

'Is it all done now, Lovejoy?' Lydia asked.

'Somebody'll tell us that, soon,' I said. 'Let's go.'

We travelled to my cottage in serene safety. No bands of

Indians lined the bypass. The old Ruby clattered un-molested into our village.

Lydia brewed up for us, then got down to repairing my clothes huffing angrily. Of course she was going to report it to the Home Secretary, the Ombudsman, and God-knows-who-else. She actually does this. She's got a file, ever-growing, of complaints about ignored complaints. I read, rested, went over past auctions.

She said nothing about the auction, but I could tell she'd been as frightened as I was. As the afternoon wore on she got me to try and make up with Sandy and Mel. I knew it was her way of wanting the world sewn together again. About five o'clock, with the sky leaden and winds rising, I phoned. Sandy screamed, 'Oh, Mel, dear! It's him! The one who said those things about our lovely motor,' and slammed the receiver down. Lydia rang and talked for twenty minutes to no avail. I was in the dogbox right enough. I tried to please her by phoning Margaret Dainty and a few of the others, even asking after Tinker. No use either.

By six o'clock the Assyrian still hadn't descended like a wolf on the fold. I was beginning to feel rather chirpy. If Big John didn't send his militia, I thought in my optimism, then he'd guessed what really happened and gone after the real villains, the gang of four. Every second that passed meant that Deamer, Chatto *et al.* were probably strapped to a table while Big John's laser beam crept nearer and nearer.

By seven o'clock I'd decided on a celebration nosh. There's a new Italian place not far, just near the Castle. Lydia protested about wasting money. She's got one of those electronic calculators that frightens me to death, but tonight I was having no ethics. There's a time and place. We drove in grandly and got the Frascati going in a corner table where the candlelight hurts your eyes.

Curiously, it was a celebration even though during the pasta bit Lydia got an attack of anxiety and the calculator appeared on the tablecloth between symbolic mounds of noodles. She reproachfully lectured us about the state of Lovejoy, Inc.'s finances. I didn't care. I've handled better reproaches than that. Electronic gadgets are no experts in the human condition, and I am. Two gentlemen, perhaps lawyers hatching a double fee, were engaged in tranquil debate. One day maybe I'll look that educated, I wished enviously.

'I think we've made it, chuckie,' I told Lydia by the dregs of the Barolo. 'We've won.' And I was bragging how brilliantly I'd pulled it all off as we left. That was when our two solicitors finished their repast and courteously stepped aside to let us proceed out of the door. You can always tell real gentlemen, I was thinking as they came after through the trellised arch into the dark street and kidnapped us.

'Keep going, Lovejoy,' one said amiably. 'Big John Sheehan needs you.'

'How dare you,' etc., etc., from Lydia.

They drove us to the Coach End Motel, five miles out of town. 'Why here?' I asked. 'Big John wouldn't be seen dead in this dump.'

'It is Mr Sheehan's,' one of the smoothies announced. Closer to, in the garish lights of the forecourt, he looked cadaverous.

'Nice place,' I said, swallowing. I hadn't known. Watching the Rolls recede towards the bypass was the loneliest feeling on earth. Many parked cars, the sound of a band, the hubbub of bars. If Ledger's police had followed they'd be daft enough to trail the Rolls into London, leaving me in Big John's hands.

'Does she never stop rabbiting?' the goons asked me as we climbed stairs. I'd looked about for doorways, crowded saloons, a dance-hall, but we went in through a side entrance. The ascent was steep, the walls bare. Lydia was shoved one-handedly on to a corridor chair. I couldn't help being interested. Maybe if I lived he'd show me how to do that. I was hauled through a door and faced a roomful of violence. The atmosphere was thick with potential assault.

Five blokes played cards in one corner, four others talked quietly. One played patience. He hadn't noticed a red nine on a black ten. Big John was in his favourite ochre, a pricey worsted. Prize thoroughbred cattle had gladly laid down their lives to provide skin for his·hand-crafted tan shoes. Troglodytes had hewed the gemstones that glittered on his cravat, his rings, his facer watch, his wristlet charm. He'd been pacing the floor. You could practically see where the carpet still smouldered. Two of the morose card-players showed signs of a recent battering. Their eyes were multiple purples, lips negroidal under brown crusted blood. Big John had expressed displeasure.

'Wotcher, John,' I said. He stood and stared.

'Shtum, you,' one of the goons told me, and said to John, 'Him and her went home to his rubbishy pad in the sticks—'

I'd have complained, but democracy had closed for the night.

'They did nothing,' the goon added. He had one of those carrying voices would-be Hamlets pray for. 'Phoned friends, nothing. Rang them two queers, nosh at the Romagna Mia. She talked about cooking and stuff, though we waited all the meal.'

'Right,' Big John said. I actually saw his gold-capped teeth gleam as he walked and belted me a backhander across the face. I went over, ruining the card player's patience and fetching up against a sofa. A bloke snickered, extended a leg and toed me away. Big John stepped across and kicked the bloke's legs once, twice, again, again, until something cracked, then strolled back to the ornate mantelpiece. He snapped his fingers. The bloke who'd kicked me was bundled out. Somebody gave Big John a thin cigar, lit it. He hadn't smoked at all, once.

'Funny tart you got, Lovejoy. You dun arf pick 'em.' He shook his head, mystified.

'They pick me, John.'

He grinned, blowing smoke. 'Sure, boyo. I remember. The CO's wife. I owe you one for that.'

We were in the same khaki mob once. I'd accidentally come forward for something when he'd been wrongly accused. It hadn't been my fault, and a woman who chats you up on a lonely railway station can be anybody from anywhere, right? I went with her once or twice—well, all right, continuously—on a forty-eight hour pass. She'd said she was divorced. How could I know?

'You owe me two, John. You hit me for nowt just now.'

'Oh, that.' He blew a pious halo in smoke, prepared to forgive and forget.

'And a third thing you owe me,' I said. 'I tried to save you a fortune, but you were too thick to realize.'

The room stood still. The band crashed and trumpeted on the floor below. The walls vibrated to merrymaking. But up here I was pig-in-the-middle. My stance was supposed to imply that everything had been done on Big John's behalf.

'Wait.' Big John gestured his men to immobility, nodded permission for me to explain. That meant I better had.

'You bought it then, eh?' I said. It was there on a baize-covered table, just as I'd seen it in the auction room. 'What's your idea of the scam, John?'

'You've used up ten of your nine lives by that, Lovejoy.' He pointed at me, two fingers with the cigar burning crossways between. 'You swapped the genuine pendant for this fake. It's even got your name on it. *Lovejoy fecit.* You always label your own forgeries, you bastard. I know that much. Too big-headed to sell without bragging, eh? So gimme Deamer's original piece, Lovejoy.'

He clouted me, other hand and different direction. This time into a plant-stand that rained leaves. The plantpot stood firm, thank God. It'd have driven me in like a tent-peg. I reeled to, dabbing at my mouth and nose. Blood. Still, nobody had kicked me this time. Things were looking up.

'Or . . .?' I prompted, crossing dizzily to an armchair, and perched with a hankie at my face. My head was spinning.

'Or what?' He was puzzled at my composure. I knew him, but he knew me.

'Or you're wrong, John. To start with, I was searched in and out. Police cameras kept a film record of my every move in that office. Ask Ledger to let you run the videos. And the thing was strapped down with a look-only grid. The only item I touched was a lens my apprentice passed me via a guard.'

Big John interrogated the galaxy about the word 'apprentice' by a raised brow. The cold voice answered, 'He means that gabby tart.'

'And your people examined it before the sale, John.'

He nodded, glowering bitterly at the two beaten men. 'All the time. So what happened?' They waited anxiously for my reply.

'Nobody replaced it, John. No dummying.'

'See, boss?' one of the puffy-faced goons said with relief.

'But there was no *Lovejoy fecit* on it until . . .' Big John paused.

'Until I put it there, pal. I used a marker loupe.'

'You marked—ruined—my frigging antique, Lovejoy?' Luckily he hesitated a split second. 'But you're a divvie. You'd never mark it, unless it was . . .'

'Fake, John.' We'd got there at last.

'She did pass him an eyeglass, John,' some idiot said.

John strolled over and abruptly stunned the speaker with a backhander. 'Then you should have told me, careless bleeder.' He paused and addressed the room. ' 'Tisn't in me heart to forgive carelessness. D'you hear me now?' The room nodded. His Londonderry brogue was showing, an ominous index of exasperation.

'The alternative theory, John,' I said, 'is that I went in and put my mark on Deamer's "original"—for no reason, at great risk and expense, while alienating all the peelers in East Anglia.'

'Or . . .?' he said. One thing about Sheehan is that he's no time for the superfluous. Bloodied as I was, I had to smile at his echo.

'Or the truth, John. You'll not like it. Anybody got a drink?'

Another nod. They got me a Spätlese, some German stuff which takes the blood taste from your tongue. It gave me a thinking minute. Then I told him the truth, the whole truth, and nothing but the truth. Nearly.

'Deamer worked up a syndicate to exploit scotchers,' I said. 'Brought from Fife, good big baroque pearls fresh out of the water. The way into the international antiques market is a variant. Even art forgers like Michaelangelo and Adolf Hitler knew that. Different degrees of sureness, of course.'

He was restless. 'Go on, Lovejoy.'

'Start off with a biggie. It could have been any famous pearls: the Florence-Marchimisi set, Naples 1871. The Dudley pearls of London. The Orange pearls. The Notch Brook freshwater pearl from New Jersey, 1857, that the Empress Eugénie acquired. Any. Deamer settled for a baroque piece, because scotchers are baroques.'

'Not always.' Big John actually said those words, but they somehow cast an image of Deamer on a meathook. I almost retched, carried bravely on.

'But usually. A lookalike of a famous baroque. The Canning Siren's so well documented every collector knows it. He got a syndicate together. Chatto, Vernon, Vernon's wife Donna. They could produce the goods, actually incorporate a big baroque in a forgery. Pearls are difficult. Gold's easy, now that every little forger does spectrography.'

'True,' Big John agreed miserably. 'It's a fucking nuisance, all this chemistry. Right?'

'Right,' the universe chorused gruffly, glaring at the very idea.

'And once Deamer's fake variant was sold as authentic, they were in. They could do it time after time. Message ends, John.'

He rose, reasoning. Something of a record, I mused. 'And every year Deamer's syndicate produces more brilliant lookalikes,' he seethed. My bruises screamed for exemption next round, please. 'Authenticity would be guaranteed—once his first item was sold at a nationally-known auction. Like today.'

'Well done,' I said and got a warning finger. I wouldn't be allowed any more liberties. 'I couldn't stand by, John. I heard of it, and tried phoning you a warning. Twice.'

His brow furrowed. Icy-Voice went white. 'And?' Big John asked.

I shrugged. This sickened me, but God knows what else I could do. 'I got told to piss off.'

Big John sauntered casually past his men, opened the window. We were two floors up. Night air drifted in to music. 'Out, Harry,' he said conversationally.

'John,' Icy-Voice pleaded, voice panic-hot.

'Go on, Lovejoy.' Big John was actually having his cigar relighted when two of his goons lurched Harry out of the window into the fragrant dark. A crash failed to interrupt Big John's train of thought, though the rest of us were drenched in sweat.

'I'll make no bones about it, John,' I said. 'I don't like Deamer. I owe him one, the bastard. When you took no notice I thought: Fine. I'll bubble Deamer with John. And I'd honestly tried.'

'So you got your apprentice to carry a marker loupe in?'

'Mmmmh. And marked Deamer's pendant. The loupe'll still be in her handbag.' I halted dramatically, close to overplaying. 'If I'd wanted entirely out, I'd have done nothing. Instead I risked all sorts of hassle from peelers to get in.'

'What'd they done to you, Lovejoy? Some bird?'

'Killed an old lady. She wasn't much, but that wasn't her fault.'

There was a long pause. One of the lawyer types made as if to speak but wisely stifled. Finally Big John cleared his throat, and pronounced.

'The point is, boys, Lovejoy is no muscle.'

All gazes fixed me with the detached curiosity of the palæontologist. Trilobites have received more humane glances.

'He has,' Big John said on, thoughtfully, 'no hopes on his own. So he could be telling the truth. Check the tart.' A goon sprang out, hardly an eddy in the smoke. 'And Lovejoy needn't have marked the wealth. Right?'

Anxiously I joined in the chorus of agreement to help it along. I was sweating trickles between my shoulder-blades. All jewellery is 'wealth' to buyer-dealers on Big John's scale.

'So you owe me, John,' I said. 'If you're too dumb to accept a favour . . .'

'I've warned you before, Lovejoy,' he said, but didn't move, which saved me a walk back from wherever he'd have clouted me. 'There's only one thing. The police . . .'

Some people do it by instinct, which is the reason Big John Sheehan's still got the whole Greek antiques market sewn-up in his brother's pocket (not his own, note. He's not daft).

'Thought you'd never get there, John.' I grinned so much my lip split again and bled merrily. 'You're right it's the police. It's Chandler. Ledger warned me off in case I mucked up his own ploy, which was to net Chandler. I reckon Chandler is in with Deamer; wanted to cop me red-handed. It would have cleared them.'

We observed the infinite while Big John caught up.

'You did well, Lovejoy. Brave lad.'

'Ah no, John.' Regretfully I shook my head. 'They've done it. Chandler stays on in the local antiques fraud division. They need him. It's unbeatable, John. You, me, my apprentice in there, we've all lost.' I shrugged, sighed to show how much it hurt.

Nobody does Big John down, as we all knew.

He paced, stopped. 'One last bit of proof, Lovejoy. Heads'll bounce for this, m'dear boy.' He was warning me that somebody was going to swing, and soon. Therefore he had to be sure.

'Will six bits do?' I offered. 'Send this army. Take flashlights. You'll find six trial replicas of Deamer's so-called antique in my workshed.'

His eyes slitted. 'Six half-dones maybe means one fully completed one, eh, Lovejoy?'

'That was my original plan, John. I admit it. Until Deamer and Chatto did for Owd Maggie. Then it got beyond a joke. And by then Deamer had framed me for another job. The Old Bill were everywhere.'

Big John pointed to three goons. 'Go. Take that bird to show where.'

'Show them where all six are, love,' I called as the door opened, meaning not to mention the seventh.

'I shall insist on a receipt, Mr Sheehan,' she called back, a threat.

It felt no safer with fewer goons around. Every one could have diced me single-handed.

While we waited I told Big John the story right from the first seance, the antiques sweep with Donna, Owd Maggie buying it, Vernon's passing, my hopeless raid on Deamer's. I was careful to include Donna's affair with Chatto, and exclude the details about the big baroque pearls to be found in the river. Let him assume they were got from the Tay. It would do no harm, especially to Vanessa.

We chatted old times while we waited. Big John was laughing and asking my opinion about Lucie-Smith's famed advice on collecting (find a group of nutters obsessed with one category of art; trust your own judgement; then *spend*) when they brought Lydia back. 'The more I see of that

Siren job,' I was telling Big John, 'the more it looks like
the work of that Italian goldsmith near the big bridge in
Florence. Know him? Does it all from photos. He has an
army of photographers, though he's mostly Etruscan items.'
They'd been an hour and fetched my six test fakes in a
brown paper bag. They left Lydia outside.

'All right, Lovejoy.' John passed me the bag. 'Not bad.
If you ever finish them, let me know. Come with me.' He
sounded tired as we went to the bar.

I was frightened, because when Big John tires of people
it's they who must compensate, and I'd nothing left to
compensate with.

'Cheers,' I said over my drink, trying to smile my cheery
bloodstained smile. 'All over now, John, eh?'

'I've spent a fortune on a dud, Lovejoy. You call that all
over?' Now we were getting down to it. 'Look, Lovejoy. As I
see it there's two problems. My money, and my reputation.'
Nobody else's problems count. 'I've been used, to set up
Deamer's scam. I don't like it. I can't squash the cheque
I've paid to Tierney's, or my name'd be mud. Dicey credit's
bad, Lovejoy.'

'True, true, John,' I agreed with sincerity.

'So Deamer must pay, in spades. That's straightforward.
But he'd still be in the saddle.'

'You're right, John.' Agreeing with Big John gives a
coward a lovely safe feeling.

Sheehan stirred. 'I can't be owed, Lovejoy. It'd rankle.
Know what I mean?'

He owed me four. 'Aye, I know what you mean.'

'Deamer has to have an accident . . .' His voice
trailed.

'Wotcher, Ledger,' I said to the man suddenly between
me and the bright light. 'Did your video-camera movies
turn out okay? Sorry there wasn't a car chase, but—'

'We got what we wanted, Lovejoy.' Ledger didn't move,
nodded. ' 'Evening, John.'

'Ledger,' said Big John, wondering how much the policeman had heard.

'Chandler is under arrest.' The admission cost Ledger blood. 'All four, in fact.'

Did he say only four? Big John wanted them accessible where they could be manhandled. I too was downcast.

'What evidence?' Big John asked.

'Tapes, photos, conversations, videos, prints.' Ledger sat heavily. 'All sewn up. Oh, Lovejoy. You've met Sergeant Thomas, I think. Any chance of a pint, John?'

'If you pay, Ledger.'

'Good evening.' Donna Vernon sat opposite me on a low stool, and all sorts of little things added up: she knew so little about the antiques game; she'd been no ally of Chandler's that time he'd hauled us in . . .

We all thought a bit. I cleared my throat. We all thought some more. She was smiling. Ledger got a pint, and a small cider for Donna.

It came to me as Big John waited. 'Vernon who got killed. He was another of yours?'

'Yes, Lovejoy,' Donna said. 'Not my husband. A fraud squad man. I realized that Chandler also suspected me when he pulled you and me in for questioning.'

'Why the sweep, then?'

'Deamer's idea to obscure the origin of the pendant. They'd have had everybody turning up and making their own.'

Ledger interposed, sensitive as a wall. 'They started suspecting Agent Vernon. Chatto did it.'

'Bastard,' I accused Ledger. 'You used me to distract attention from her.'

Ledger smirked. 'Yes. My idea, that. Playing on Chatto's superstition.'

'And to collar them?'

He beamed. 'You were a big help, Lovejoy. Donna was on the cameras. She's on the antiques squad too. She realized what you'd done.'

'You were so slick we missed it first time of viewing,' she said.

'You didn't point it out to Chandler, I suppose?'

'Ah no,' Ledger said, pulling a face over his drink. 'We lied, told him you'd lodged a complaint that it was a fake. We told Chandler that Deamer had kept his prize piece for himself.'

'He rowed with Olivia in his car,' Donna said. 'We've it all on video.'

I said, 'Do I get paid?'

'You have the satisfaction of helping justice, Lovejoy,' Ledger chuckled. 'The proper way. Saves you persuading John here to murder them all for you.'

'If you'd hauled Deamer earlier, Ledger,' I said, 'there'd be two others celebrating here.'

'Shut it, Lovejoy,' Ledger shot back. 'Misjudgement's not your prerogative. We were identifying the whole syndicate, collecting evidence.'

Big John was looking thoughtfully at the pendant. It was worth only its materials now, not the fortune he'd paid. He'd still lost.

'Ledger,' he said suddenly. 'Any chance of seeing Deamer? Not for anything in particular. In return I'll help you to collect evidence. Put your boys with him while I ask it. Ten seconds.'

'Deal,' Ledger said. 'Call off those villains you left sawing shotguns upstairs.'

'Deal,' said Big John.

'Then there were two.' Donna didn't smile at my remark as Big John and Ledger departed, emanating mutual mistrust.

'See you home, Lovejoy?' she asked, smiling. 'We were lovers once. In the circumstances a little stroll's the least I can expect.'

'In the circumstances, love,' I said gently, 'it's the most.'

CHAPTER 29

'Quite like old times,' I cracked in Donna's motor.

'What's Big John up to?' Donna mused. She had the woman motorist's habit of ten tennis glances at each intersection while fiddling the gearstick. It always drives me mad. 'A charity call on Prisoner Deamer's the last thing I'd have thought.'

So that was her reason. Once a peeler always a peeler. I knew what John would ask Deamer, but I wasn't telling Donna. She drove towards my village.

'I know you must think me hateful, Lovejoy,' she began when I said nothing. 'They were suspicious of Sid Vernon. Probably he'd been a plant too long. I was brought in as Vernon's wife to keep the surveillance going.'

I didn't say Chatto must have been pleased. By a whisker.

'That night when—' she actually seemed to colour up a little; if she hadn't been in the fraud mob I'd have suspected tenderness— 'when Vernon was murdered, was supposed to be the night Ledger closed in. We still don't know how Deamer got wind about Sid. While I was in the bedroom alone, afterwards, I was signalled that the planned raid on Deamer's was off because Vernon hadn't come. We learned he was dead. So surveillance had to go on.'

'With me framed, blamed, maimed . . .'

'You were quite safe, Lovejoy,' she said earnestly.

'The hangman always says it won't hurt, love. Nobody's ever verified it.'

'Now, Lovejoy—'

'Now, Sergeant. Hadn't you thought of protecting Owd Maggie?'

'That was an unfortunate oversight.' Green tears showed in her eyes from the dashboard's glow. She was snuffling one-handed into her hankie as we arrived and halted on my gravel. God, I was glad to be home and done with the lot of them. Bluntly I told her so. Boot a bleating bobby, I always say.

'You're determined to misunderstand, Lovejoy. That night I didn't have to make love. Oh, I know you're unreliable, a villain, unpredictable. But when I saw how you love those old things so, I began to wonder what love itself is.'

'And you wanted in.' I got out, inhaled my garden's night smog. 'You make me laugh, Sergeant. Love needs making, or there isn't any. You can't just suddenly decide to lie back and accept it as a gift from outer space. You must build, slog, labour at it, or you've got none. Create love, or go without.'

'I know that now, Lovejoy.'

'Sergeant,' I said wearily. 'Get lost.'

She was doing things to her face from a powder compact. 'Very well, Lovejoy. Whatever you wish. You've taught me something. Determination's also an essential factor.' She clicked the compact shut and dowsed the car's courtesy light. 'You will be called for at oh eight hundred hours tomorrow, and be signed over into my protective custody.'

'Me?' I shuffled uneasily. 'You can't.'

'I'll have the warrant in four hours.' Her voice held a tranquil certainty. 'You're a valuable witness.'

'Not any more.'

'But I'll swear blind that you are, Lovejoy. I'm still an officer in an important murder-and-deception case. I simply haven't time for hearts-and-flowers, waiting by the phone.'

'There's plenty of time. Ledger said so.'

'That simpering Medusa bitch of an apprentice doesn't quite see it like that, Lovejoy. She'd crump any woman who swings on your gate. And that tart Michaela French has resurfaced. I tap your phone, and she's phoning on the hour. She has money and all the crudity of her breed. She'll have to go. And your police file records many others; Margaret Dainty with her homely little act, for one. Shall I list them, in case you've forgotten?'

'Look, Donna. Let's discuss . . .'

'Eight, Lovejoy.' She reversed quickly and zoomed up the lane.

The phone was ringing. It was Big John. 'This phone's tapped, John. Get off the line.'

'Doesn't matter now, me boy,' He was Ulster jubilant. 'I've a proposition.'

'The answer's no, John. Your propositions end up with me being thumped, owed—'

'You don't know what my proposition is, boyo.'

'Aye, I do. You've seen Deamer. In return for selling you the river rights you'll pay him a huge sum to buy him the best lawyers on earth for his coming trial. If Deamer hadn't agreed to sell he'd have been found one morning accidentally hanged in his cell, right? *That's* why I won't manufacture fakes for you, John. For Deamer read Lovejoy.'

'Here, Lovejoy. Be fucking careful what you say.'

'Deamer told that loony Chatto to kill Vernon and Owd Maggie. They shouldn't *be* helped. They should be smacked for being naughty.' I slammed the receiver down trying to sound decisive, but in reality very worried. Sheehan would be after me now. He'd somehow realized about the river pearls and saw himself as the new owner of Deamer's scam. All he needed was a good forger who knew antique jewellery, and he was on the way to owning the universe. He needed me.

Deciding to run for it's easy. Getting going's the hard part. I was rummaging for a clean shirt when the phone rang. Sandy, a-squeal with excitement. There's no peace.

'Not now, Sandy,' I said tiredly. I had a long way to go. God knows where.

'Listen, I mean it's a fantabulissimo *chance*, Lovejoy!' His voice was a screech. 'You make absolutely countless dinkie-sweet antique jewellery with pearls from Big John's river oh he's such a *barbarian* and my Mel and yours truly get a *monopoly* marketing—'

'Sandy, I've had it up to here. Cheers.' I dropped the receiver. Somewhere there must be sanctuary.

Quickly I wolfed some bread and cheese and coffee and plodded out. Where to? I'd a vague notion of heading north, but reflex took over and I found myself trudging down through the darkness towards the distant string of orange lights on the far side of the valley. A lift on the bypass down to the harbour took a whole hour in coming, even with the heavy traffic thickening before midnight.

Beatrice was in, unsteady and anxious and hiccoughing. I explained my predicament.

'Just one day, Bea,' I pleaded, lying. I meant longer. 'Owd Maggie always said I could depend on you.'

'Not here, sweetie. Barney's due any minute. He's only seeing a coaster out.'

'Is there nowhere?'

'Let me think.' She stood on the stairs, swaying. I didn't know if it was booze or a trance. 'My friend has a caravan out on the point.'

'By the Martello tower?'

'Yes. It's empty for a week. She told me yesterday that the people renting it can't come. Will that do?'

She was in no fit state to drive me down, so after a few innuendoes about settling the rent in kind I walked the cobbled wharf following the curved line of shore lamps towards the old tower's red marker beacon. They light them for foolish aircraft. I reached it in an hour.

The caravan smelled musty and sounded hollow, but it had a gas stove, a shoebox-sized fridge containing essential grub, and electric light. I made the bed, smiling at Bea's alcoholic suggestiveness, promising to 'bring your milk as soon as the harbour starts moving, darling'. I went to the door and stood looking out into the dark freshness. I'd made

it. Refuge. Bea wouldn't tell. Cardew and Seth were the
only two others in the know, and they needed a spiritual-
ist to broadcast even a burp. I was safe, on my own at
last.

The night was tranquil. That was the word. Tranquil.
You wouldn't think that an innocent scene could be anything
but serene, could you? Yet it had all happened within a few
miles. I walked round, stared out some more. Walked round
again. I whistled a tune. *Scarborough Fayre,* by some mis-
chance.

The sea shushed to and fro less than twenty yards off.
The old tower had been erected on the end of a spit of
reinforced sand projecting from . . . Uneasily I strolled out
and prodded with my toe. Sand. Projecting from the shore.
There's quite a lot of hazy illumination along the coast. By
it I could see where I was. My lonely caravan refuge, its
cheerful electric light shining, was quite definitely situated
between the salt water and the sea sand. I stopped
whistling.

Now, I'm honestly not superstitious. That's ridiculous.
And I'm the last bloke in the world to get spooked. So I
wasn't at all worried. Of course not. I don't lose my cool.
Oh, I admit I sat on the sand and looked at the damned
place more closely. Nothing wrong with that, is there? I'd
got to live here, after all.

'Are you the refuge I really want, Cockalorum?' I asked
it aloud, and sat throwing pebbles at the sea.

Out there, a sound grew. It was centred on a light. One,
then two lights. A red. A green. Then a third, whitish yellow.
A small boat. The lights aligned, separated. The sound was
louder. A boat engine, coming closer. I threw a pebble.
Another. Plop.

Well, it was either scarper or wait. And I was too tired
to do any more running. If it was Donna, just too bad.
Michaela was unlikely. Big John was probable. Barney,
irate at yet another nocturnal visit from me to Bea, was a

possibility. Lydia was six-to-four against, say. Margaret no chance. Helen . . .

I used up a handful of pebbles. Plop. Plop. Nowhere to go, and bats of memory haunting my mind.

The boat grated on the shingle, its engine coughing. 'Hello, Lovejoy.'

'Wotcher, Vanessa.'

She leaped and splashed expertly, standing there holding the rope. 'I'd an idea it was you. Everybody's talking of the auction at the pub. Billy saw the caravan lights. Nobody's supposed to use it this week.'

'Word travels fast.'

'We all know Beatrice's friend owns it.' She scuffed shingle with one shoe. 'You sound all in, Lovejoy.'

'I'm okay.' A pause.

'Are you sure you really want to stay here?'

'It's the last place on earth.' I tried to sound carefree. It came out as a kind of whine. I'm pathetic.

'Well, then. My place isn't palatial, but you're more than welcome, Lovejoy.'

'Ta, love.' I got up, brushed the sand off and climbed into her boat. The caravan looked lonely and vulnerable there on the sloping shingle. Vanessa went to dowse the lights and pushed us off.

We puttered slowly away from the tower's red light. Looking at Vanessa's hair, blowing red and green in the boat's lamps, I couldn't help thinking. Tom her dad still longed for his gamekeeper's job along the riverside estate. Now Big John owned it; he needed an experienced keeper. If I went in with Big John's scam—only if, mind—then I could swing jobs for the two of them. Sheehan wouldn't have a clue about freshwater pearling . . .

Moon showed from behind a cloud. Vanessa's hair silvered.

. . . And supervision was minimal. I could control the output of forgeries. Plus a percentage cut from Tom and

Herbie. Tinker would be especially keen. Risky, of course, because you didn't cross Big John without incurring considerable displeasure. But the bastard owed me, didn't he?

I'd have to stay on the right side of my rescuer, though, until I'd got it all organized. I smiled at Vanessa in the iridescent moonlight, hoping I'd done my teeth so they showed clean and that my lip didn't bleed again.

'Penny for your thoughts, Lovejoy,' she said quietly.

I cleared my throat. 'Just thinking how lovely you look,' I said. 'Isn't moonlight romantic?'